AF225972

YESTERYEAR

Skylar J. Jerkins

<u>**For Myself**</u>

You will always be there waiting in the dark corner of the room, crawling towards the light as it calls out your name. As it does when it's time for anyone else to join the land of the everlasting sun. Where the land is clean and whole, such as all life should be.

CHAPTER ONE

I remember the beach. The sound it made when it crashed upon the shoreline. I finish writing as the nurse calls my name; I look up to see a moderately attractive woman and slowly get up and look about the room. Only three people are in this room, and only one is here for a good reason. That would be the gothic high school teen in the corner next to the television watching Full House. I look above her, noticing an old Vincent Van Gogh painting of what I believe is a mailman, but I could be wrong. I turn to the nurse.

"Is that an original?" I ask, pointing at the painting; the nurse answers by shaking her head. "I didn't think so," I say as I lean over and get my notebook. I fold the notebook in half and fit it into my back pocket. I put the pen in the front left and my phone, which has no service, social media, or calls to forward or make. It's just a black box at the bottom of a sack attached to my blue jeans; that's quite poetic in a weird way. The nurse turns in a showmanship fashion leading me down the aisle to receive my brand-new car! Kind of an odd reference to a television program to be thinking of, but the situation is weird. I stroll, counting my steps; I never realize why I do that. Trying to keep track of the ten seconds between each step, crushing any chance of a potential ecosystem between atoms. Purely because atoms are the building blocks of life.

I walk into the room; a sofa sits against the wall. Above that sofa is another Van Gogh. This one is the Starry Night, a beautiful colleague of color and a town's pure beauty in the dead of night. Beside the sofa is a little table with a lamp and a glass cup filled with peppermint. Sounds of nature are playing from a speaker below the main door. Like my classroom, the desk is clean and simple with a computer, nothing too rambunctious or monotone. The room's painted light green, carrying a melancholy peace. In front of the sofa is a glass table. The floorboards are made of mahogany and made no sound when I stepped upon them. I walk over and stare through the open blinds at the outside world; two children are playing with a red ball across the street, and next door, the neighbor is trimming his hedges. Perfect. I think, closing my eyes and feeling the sun's heat through the window. The door closes. I turned to the sound and was pleasantly greeted by a short, stout woman with short blond straight hair and a broad smile, and she, too, carried her notebook. I welcome her, take my notebook out of my pocket, sit behind the glass table, and fold the notebook between my hands.

"You must be Samuel," she says, nestling into her work chair.

"That's me," I say, raising my hand half haphazardly. "I don't quite know how to pronounce your last name yet, so give me a quick rundown, would you?" I say, chuckling.

"The first part of my last name is pronounced exactly how you read it, Gwen, and the t-o-n is pronounced town, and skey is just skey," she says reassuringly.

"So Gwen-ton-skey, Dr. Gwentonskey?" I say questioningly.

"That's it, but for the foreseeable future, you can call me Sharlin," she says with a smile. I chuckle. "For our first exercise, I would like you to introduce yourself in your own words. Then, I would like you to tell me something about yourself and your work," she says. I guess that's where it all starts. I tell myself that you must tell the therapist who you are at the beginning of therapy. How is this possible when I have no clue who I am anymore?

"My name is Samuel James Dark, and I'm a high school teacher here in Lincoln," I say, thinking that is all she wanted to hear. I begin to rub my thumb over the paper-thin cardboard. Then, carving circles with my nails. Please don't ask me about the notebook, anything but the notebook.

"Did you always want to become a teacher?" she asks.

"No, to tell you the truth, I never found out what I wanted to be. I never found out who I wanted to be," I say solemnly, thinking of Brittany and the kids. Brittany has grown distant since the board sent me home on mental leave. I believe she is contemplating divorce; that would be the cherry on top. So, I didn't care for the break, and I don't care for this, whatever you want to call it. But it was Brittany's idea, so I might as well do as she says while I still have her.

"You seem self-aware that you haven't found your place in this life," she says, locking her fingers together. "I assure you everyone has a place," she says. So sure of herself, I almost believed her there for a second.

"I guess you could say that I never bothered to care," I say, dropping the notebook; I quickly pick it up and dust it off. I hear Sharlin say something, but I can't discern the words. Finally, I look up. "Excuse me?" I put the pen back in between the pages.

"Can I see that notebook?" I fold the notebook and hold it tight against my chest.

"No, I'm not ready for anyone to see it," I say shakingly.

"All right, but when you're ready, I want to see it," she says. "Can you at least tell me what you write?" she asks curiously. I take a moment to calm myself and look up at the woman.

"Stories," I say coldly.

"What kind of stories?" she asks, tilting her head as if to study my demeanor.

"The kind that ain't worth looking through a telescope to find," I say. Why would you tell Sharlin you, bastard? I think to myself.

"Can you write me something for tomorrow's session?" she says, pointing to her calendar. I look at her, questioning her intent for this exercise, but I'll follow along. Honestly, at this point, I'll do anything to get back into working again, and I nod, agreeing.

"What would you like for me to write?" I say, looking down at the notebook's purple covering, the only border between its creator and the material used to create it.

"I want you to write your story, not you in the past or the future, but you know, just you," she says, pointing at me. I agree, and we spend the rest of the session doing breathing exercises that bring warmth to my stomach that make me feel slightly at ease. Before leaving, she reminds me that our next session is at five tomorrow evening, giving me time to work on my story. I wave to the woman behind the desk and head out the door. I carefully take one step at a time because that one step could end my life. I'm superstitious like that. Once on the cement, I look around and notice the clouds are now gray, the color of storms and death. I decide to walk a little down the street to a bus stop and sit beside a homeless man with a sign that reads, "THE END TIMES ARE COMING" ignoring this, I huff as I stand. The notebook falls out of my hands. As I bend over to get the notebook, someone steps on one of the open pages and rips it in half.

"Hey!" I call out to the businessman walking down the street—the same businessman who pulled one of the pages, which is still stuck to his shoe. I walked after him. "Sir, wait!" I say, breaking into a brisk fast-paced speed walk. I rushed past the man and blocked him from crossing another street, causing us to bump into one another and send me to the ground. The notebook falls inches away from my fingertips. He was a tall, bulky man with singed blond hair, quite the opposite of me, who had no muscle to count for with my short, put-off-to-side haircut, which needed some trimming. I realized that some of it hung just short of my eyelids. I look at this man nervously.

"I'm sorry to bother you, but you have something that belongs to me," I say, pointing down and showing him the piece of paper stuck to his excellent and shiny black shoes.

"Oh, dear boy, my apologies. Let me get that for you, and we can go out for a nice cold beer," the man says, taking the piece of paper from his shoe, taking the notebook, and neatly placing it perfectly where it should be. "Let's head off then," the man says, putting his heavy right arm over my shoulder and leading me to the nearest bar just two blocks away from the main strip of the walkway. The bar was called The Pub (very basic yet very mysterious). The neon light was shining a bright purple color, reflecting off our cool crisp skin, the man with his clean-shaven jawline, and my neatly trimmed beard. The man gives the guard his VIP ticket, and the guard unlatches the gold lock attached to a lovely silk-red belt between two solid gold poles.

"I'm a bit underdressed for this type of place." The man looks back at me and looks me up and down. I'm wearing a nice arctic white button-down with a blood-red tie, plain black slacks, and some dress shoes (the kind you wear to church). The man smiles brightly, the purple light bouncing off his clean white teeth.

"No, my boy, you dress just fine," I hesitated. Still, as if I have been changed into a statue, he walks in without me. I look at the line of people once filled with wannabe models and actors; everyone in the bar had vanished, leaving nothing but me and the rotating door. I reach out to touch this door and push it forward, watching as the glass reflects the neon light, my face distorted as my reflection passes by. I take a sharp breath and walk through the rotating door with my eyes closed and tight. I feel an incredible rush of wind which causes goosebumps to jump from my skin as I breathe in fresh, clean air handling something cold and wet rise and fall against my lower legs. I open my eyes and look behind me, seeing the door has dissipated. For a moment, I feel the sensation of fear, and I look around me, seeing a beach with another person sitting at the base of the dunes. There is something peculiar about those sands, almost as if they are alive. This person, blocked by the sun's brightness, rests at the top of the ridge. This aberration looks up, and I sink into the ocean. Salt water begins to fill my lungs as I am dragged deeper. I close my eyes.

"Sir!" I open my eyes and quickly shut the left as it screams in pain. What a shame that was my good eye. I open my right to see a group of people surrounding me. I turn my head a little and see more people. I think they only seem to care when someone is hurt. I had always thought this because that is the harsh truth; people only pretend to care when something is wrong with another human being, which is how the world works. My nose hurts and is probably broken. So I realize as I breathe, feeling the curve as the air goes through my nostril cavity. The girl kneeling beside me wore a pink flannel turtleneck. She looked as if she had just gotten off from school. I bet she didn't think this would be the most exciting part of her day, but it probably wasn't. "All right, give the guy some space, people," says the tall, lengthy man wearing a checkered vest, blue jeans, and the most expensive pair of Air Jordans I have ever witnessed. Some of the crowd does as the man says and goes about their day. "If he ain't dead, don't worry about him," I hear someone say, which might just be my mind playing tricks on me. The girl goes to touch my face with her tiny hands. I wince and sit up, crawling backward only a few inches.

"It's okay," she says, her voice not nearly a whisper. Yet, I can still hear it over the commotion of babies crying and cars crashing into one another. Some women down the strip complained about the weather being too cold. This woman may be older than I am. "I'm just going to fix your nose exactly how it was," she says lightly, grabbing my face; her hands are relaxed and soft against my skin. I close my eyes. *"Pop,"* I hissed in pain, flaring my nostrils. I look at myself in the window of a dress shop. In that window is a display of a stunning blue dress. Putting my focus on myself, I see that I am beginning to grow what is perceived as a black eye, and my nose is blooded. Looking down and seeing little droplets of blood smearing down my shirt, I begin to worry. Where is my notebook? I ask myself as I search the ground. I look up at the window again, seeing the girl with the pink turtle neck still beside me, flipping through the notebook. People walk around us calling us names I don't care to mention. Through the crowd, I finally spoke to this girl.

"Can I have that back, please?" I say, holding my hand as if expecting her to lay it down. "I'm not very used to people looking at it," I say, folding my arms and looking around to see if anything would take my attention. I find nothing and realize that it's pointless to practice, trying to find something other than what you want or are going to get. It all just ends with you searching for more.

"Sure, can I finish this real quick?" I nod, agreeing. She must have seen that I was uncomfortable since she finished the poem early. The verse she reads is about a lonesome merchantman trapped inside a house in the depth of winter. "I like that," she says sweetly, handing over the notebook.

"Thank you," I say timidly, afraid of getting off the ground and dusting myself off. Unsure of what to do, I decided to help the young lady catch her bearings.

"What does it mean?" she asks as I turn to leave, clutching the notebook so tightly my knuckles turn white. I hesitate as if I'm frozen, stuck here at this moment. Then, after a moment of absolute fear, I look down as I face her.

"It means nothing. There is no point to the story or the man who wrote it," I say, turning back around and briskly walking down the sidewalk uncaringly. I don't even count the seconds between each step as

I run to the end of the walkway and turn to rush down the stairs into the underground railway station. I quickly bought my ticket for forty dollars (I spent what was left of the one hundred my wife gave me before heading out). I look at the steps as if looking for someone to follow me. Yet, I find that the only thing walking on those steps are other customers going to and from their final destination. There is a metaphor for death in that realization I begin to realize as I go into the train and take my seat furthest to the door and closest to the emergency brakes. If I did pull that lever, what would I be saving? Certainly not myself. I take my pen from my pocket and lay the notebook on the hardened seat with an old pizza stain. I open the notebook to a blank page and think of a title for my personalized story.

Yesteryear, I wrote.

I etch down a few blue lines. I should call my wife, I think to myself, accidentally writing my thoughts. I tear the page out and throw it into a neighboring seat; I get out my phone and realize again that it is out of service. How do you, of all people, forget your phone has no benefit, you stupid bastard? Going to the back of the train and opening an old yellow box with a rusted-over phone symbol on the front. I open the door seeing the wires popping out of the bottom of the box. The wire connected to the receiver is still intact. I get out my loose change, pay the twenty-five cents, and dial our home number; it rings for centuries until I hear the static clatter of the phone being picked up from the other end. My son Alex speaks as I hear Brittany shouting from the kitchen.

"Hello?" Alex says. I grin widely—such curiosity from such an innocent mind.

"Hey Alex, it's daddy!" I say with false enthusiasm. Sure, it's good to hear your kids get so excited at your arrival, but how long will that excitement last? That's the one question I have always resented asking. How long until they grow to hate you? I look at myself in the glass covered by graffiti and scratch marks. How long does it take for one to realize they hate themselves? How long? How long, indeed.

"Daddy!" I hear my daughter Sarah's screams coming into the living room; I can hear her snatch it out of her younger brother's hands. He gladly takes it like a champ, and I listen to him walking away. "Are you going to be late for dinner again?" I can almost picture the pout on her lip. I chuckle a little, amazed at my daughter keeping up with the time we are away from each other. Now that is dedication.

"No honey, daddy's going to be right on time for the spaghetti," I say with a bright smile that could light a room on fire. I need to buy bread from the market. I remind myself, "hey can you give the phone to mommy for me?" I ask. Sarah screams so loudly that I have to move the phone away from my ear a few inches. Jesus, I say under my breath, bringing the phone back to my ear and hearing my wife's feet stomp as she enters the living room. She thanks Sarah and tells them to play in their separate rooms. I hear my daughter's hands leave the phone, passing it to Brittany's.

"Hello?" she asks in her beautiful hazy voice. I can almost picture her staring back as I look through the window as bright lights pass at high speeds. I lose my place in the never-ending book of thought for a moment. I like to think your thoughts and memories are the only things you keep after death.

"Hey, hun. It's me," I say, looking around and seeing lines of buildings big and small pass by. The train slows, coming to its first stop, and five passengers depart. I notice a woman wearing a brown leather jacket carrying what appears to be a movie script. I cover the bottom of the phone and wish the woman good luck at her audition. She shows her appreciation by throwing the bird sky high; I uncover the speaker and only listen to the endings of my wife's sentence. "I'm sorry, Brittany, there was this actor on the train," I say with a smile (I always thought the term actress was very demeaning). She answers with a half-hearted "Wow," but I can sense the curiosity in her voice. "Yeah, so I was just calling to make sure you and the kids know I'll be home on time tonight," I say as the train leaves the station.

"Good; we missed you," she says, ending the call; I put the phone back on its hanger, close the yellow door, walk over to my seat, and pick up my notebook and pen.

Tuesday: Way back Yesteryear. I momentarily scratch out the sentence, ripping the paper and writing a new one on the next page.

Tuesday: Way back Yesteryear, this version looks much more perfect because of the curve I add to the T for Tuesday. I do the same for the W and the Y for the words Way and Yesteryear. Small details in writing make up a good read. I close the notebook. Yesteryear has to be perfect to me, even though the writer himself is far from that. I nod as if agreeing to something someone has said and wait patiently for the next stop.

CHAPTER TWO

*T**he little boy wearing blue sits in his father's old chair soaked in blood, causing his shirt to discolor into a dark brown stain on the chair.* I sign my name on the bottom, pleased with my work. Yesteryear may not be the story of my life, but it's sure to be a good tale. Finally, the train stopped in my hometown. Blackwater is a small community of houses and gas stations in the middle of nowhere that no one has ever heard of. The town has a little over four hundred population, far less than the city. Still, we beat out Clarkson (a moderately sized commune neighboring our own), which has two hundred. I stumble as I step out of the train bumping into a pedestrian who tells me to watch out for where you're going. You fuck! He seemed to have been having a bad day today; then again, we all are; it's just a matter of time until we all realize it.

"Sorry," I say quickly, dusting myself off and continuing down the stairs. I walk along the sidewalk a little past the general store, which has a sign that reads **DRINKS ARE NOW 70% TODAY ONLY!** I skimmed it and looked back down at my feet, sure not to step on any cracks to not break my mother's back. Even two years ago, she was sent six feet deep in a dark brown box, hidden away from the world under piles of dirt and never seen again by the living (not unless you're a grave robber, of course). I continue my walk until I get to Billy Freeman's house. Good old Billy is a cheap bastard with a beer belly, wears a red trucker hat, and often wears long sleeves and blue jeans (your standard redneck white American). But, with all his faults, he is an excellent friend. He used to be. As I look around, I remind myself that his lawn needs a good trim. I can't tell. Still, I think a pink bike is hidden between where the tree sits at the corner of their molded picket fence and where the wooden play area broke down some years ago. I remember their kids being heartbroken when they saw that old yellow slide resting on top of the old play area when the storm of 2022 happened. Their kids are all grown up now, and Billy got a divorce from Sandy a few months before the reckoning after everything went to shit. That's part of why I'm here, he was broken when Sandy left, and sometimes you just need a friend. I like being there for my friends, even if they are never there for me. I never cared and still don't.

I walk on the cracks of the broken walkway that had once been purified with colors. I looked over to the side of the house and saw that a blanket of rust still covered Billy's old truck. The left headlight was shattered, hanging out from where it should rest. The car is a 1990 ford F-150 and used to be a bright red. Funny how time takes a toll on the things we don't take care of, I think to myself as I put my left foot on the first step and move it quickly, seeing that the brick is broken and my foot would have gone through. I take a sharp breath, continue up the stairs, and open the screen door. I knock three times and wait. Finally, after a few moments of waiting, I close the screen door and walk over to the lip of the final step. I block my eyes from the sun and look at the sky seeing gray boulders. These clouds slowly inch their way over this little town.

"That could be a problem," I say to myself, checking the time on my watch, 1:40 PM which means I still have at least two hours before dinner. I go back to the screen door, open it and knock on the door another three times, calling out to Billy. Finally, I go to the window and see the curtains are closed. I walk to the door, hearing my shoe click as I stomp over the mahogany slab, blocking me from getting to my friend.

"Billy, you in there?!" I yell, cupping my hands over my mouth like a megaphone. I rest my ear against the front door to see if I can hear any movement. I don't hear anything besides Billy's old vinyl player. The song Forever by the 1960s band The Marvelettes. A perfect piece about how much a woman is willing to sacrifice to be with her lover. There is a dark side to the song, however. That dark side, the woman, could be forced to be how she describes being the "fool" in tune. Her partner could be the decisive figure forcing her to comply with his wishes. I knock three more, slamming my fist against the door as hard as possible, screaming the man's name. After another few moments, I looked out into the street and the neighbor's yard seeing no one out on this fine rainy day. I turned back to the door and decided to try turning the golden door knob and pushing.

I entered the living room, found his kitchen chair, and turned onto its side. I bring it back to its feet; I dust off the seat, pick it up from the bottom, and take it into the kitchen. I push it under the table and look at the three dusty chairs with the first letters of his family's names engraved into the wood. I close my eyes and run my fingers over each carving, feeling the curve of the letters. Perfect. As I open my eyes and go into his study, I look around, seeing the walls of books old and unkempt. I look over to the corner of the room where he usually works and carefully examine the available novels and bifocals of senior scientists and philosophers. Billy had always kept the brains for a successful career in philosophy and science but never could get the start he deserved. That goes for both of us. I have the potential to become a fruitful poet or even a novelist. Still, I settled for being a Psychology teacher. That was the worst mistake I could ever make. That no longer matters, though.

I run my hands over pieces of paper that hold Billy's thoughts and opinions of what happens after death or what's out there in the universe; we've talked about these things while having a beer and breathing whatever we can get high off of through a bong in college. Finally, I picked up one piece of paper folded in half as if it were meant to fit into an envelope. I flip it over and see the heading; it seems like this letter is to me. I open the letter and begin to read out loud, which has become a bad habit from reading the kids' bedtime stories.

"Dear Samuel. I now see the truth as it is and how it will always be. This world is a terrible old friend and will always be terrible. Since the divorce, I have grown lonely, and I thank you for your company while I was in a dark place. Getting married was the best thing that could have happened to me because I was finally happy. So where does that leave me now?" I don't know my old friend. I think, putting the letter into the left front pocket and walking out into the hallway. I look down the corridor and see that his door is closed. I turn my head terrified of what I might find. Maybe he needed help or didn't. Either way, he is in a far better place than we deserve. I run my hand over the railing as I walk down the stairs knocking off old dust bunnies and dirt. Once I reach downstairs, I walk over to the table, open my notebook, and prepare my pen; I press it onto the paper and begin writing.

Billy's story, much like mine, has its ups and downs. The difference between us is that he made something out of his gift, and as I write goodbye in my own words, it's not really goodbye, more of just an ending to the man's story. *After a while, the little boy blue sets his fathers' old red chair aflame, watching as the fire spreads throughout the house and onto the ceiling. He takes this moment and goes into the restroom and says to himself. Farewell as the sun's blistering flames overtake his body.* I rest the paper on the kitchen table's center, walk into the living room, and remove the needle from the record. No longer anyone here to listen to you anymore, old girl. Putting the old vinyl in its casing, resting it in Sandy's favorite red chair's seat, and walking out of the house.

I get a few blocks from the place before breaking down in tears as I walk the other two miles that separate me from where I used to call home.

This part of town has always had this unsettling gray feel to it. The general store to the right is owned by a German man named Peter, which is very fitting considering his face and stature. This town used to have a movie rental store, but it was shut down sometime last year because the owner had been accused of selling weed to underage children. These allegations were false, but the trial later led to the business going under, taking the owner along with it. I never knew the owner's name or where he is now. His story is interesting because what happened is the exact opposite of what Billy's philosophy was based around. I remember him saying to me one day, "They only remember you when you are gone" there is some truth behind this; I will always remember Billy for the good man he was, yet the world will never know this. That is the sad truth behind it all; even if you are remembered, it won't last forever. I continue to walk, passing some pedestrians with sadness screaming from their pores into the world, fluttering like butterflies in the air in peaceful bliss. I look up, covering my eyes, and see a storm coming about. Looking back down, I begin to run. It started to rain once I reached the strip my house sits on. I reached behind my back, untucked my shirt, and hid the notebook under it, hugging it close to my chest.

Blinded by the rain, I bump into a pedestrian, tell them I'm sorry, and continue running until I have reached our house's driveway. I slowly walk up the blacktop and stairs twice and knock on the door. She usually answers on the second knock, but the rainfall silences her voice. Finally, Brittany opens the door, noticing the bloodshot in my eyes, and lets me in. I walk into the house and look into the living station seeing that the kids are both fast asleep watching Barny the purple Dinosaur. I don't have to look to know the high-pitched graze voice. I see Brittany folding her arms as if looking for an answer.

"What?" I say, slowly walking into the kitchen, leaving a water trail on the hardwood flooring. I listen as water falls from the hem of my shirt.

Finally, I reach the kitchen and set the notebook softly on the table. I open the refrigerator door and grab a beer bottle.

"I thought you said you would quit," she says, closing the door behind me. I go over to the silverware cabinet, get out a bottle opener, open the bottle over the sink, and lazily throw the opener into the cabinet along with the knives. I pull out a chair and sit down, letting the waterfall from my matted wet hair. I take a long sip, letting the liquor burn the back of my throat. I set the bottle down, leaning forward, and began to cry. My voice is broken and horsey as I try speaking.

"I'm trying, Brit. I am," I say, looking up at her; she gets down and rubs my back softly. "I'm sorry I made you and the kids worry," I say sobbingly. She looks at me in fear, and I scream, throwing the bottle against the wall, crashing, leaving a brownish liquid against the light blue wall as it slowly slithers down.

"Samuel!" she screams, running into the living room and bringing Alex into the kitchen "what's gotten into you?" she says, holding the boy close to her breast and running her hands through his dark brown hair, his eyelashes jump and fall slowly back to slumber.

"I" silenced myself to think of my following few words carefully. "I'm sorry," I say and get off the seat. I walk into the living room, seeing that Sarah is at peace. I pick her up; she wakes momentarily and rests her head on my shoulder. Perfect. I say, looking at her little face between my neck and shoulder. I slowly walk back into the kitchen. "You take him. I take her," I whisper. She nods and tells me under her breath that we will come back into the living room. I nod regrettably and let her go into the kids' bedroom first. She steps over Alex's red fire truck. He has always been fascinated with trucks and cars to the point that he has helped me maintain our minivan. I smile, remembering when he did his first oil check almost a year ago. My mind went straight to the gutter when he said, "Dad, help me get it out." That was a good memory. A perfect memory. I walk over to Sarah's bed and untuck her My Little Pony covers halfway down to the foot of the bed. I don't see her, but Brittany stands behind me, holding back a smile. I cover Sarah up and kiss her forehead. Brittany and I take a moment to look at one another and walk out into the living room. I grab the remote and turn off the television. I sit it on the little cabinet close to the recliner, a few feet from the living room, and enter the kitchen. A few feet from the front door sits a china cabinet filled with old ceramic ducks and glass women's shoes; in the center rests a picture of our little family, so beautiful but far from perfect. Then again, searching for perfection is a fool's game. Sometimes it finds you when you least expect it. Yes, I do believe so.

Brittany goes over, sits on the sofa, and pats the cushion closest to the end, which is entirely understandable, considering I had just come through those doors smelling like rainwater a few moments ago. I sit down, uneasy and fearful of what she might say.

"Have you eaten anything?" She asks, checking her nails; she huffs in aggravation, walks over to the television stand, and gets out a pink nail file, rubbing it against her nails, sharpening them. I put my head back down, looking at the notebook; the black and white design is beginning to fade away, like dust in the wind.

"No," I say hesitantly, getting off the couch.

"Are you going to tell me where you have been?" She asks, opening the cabinet door and tossing the file back into its deep dark cubby. I look up at her. "What happened to your eye?" she says worryingly. She rushes over and places her hands against my checks. I wince in pain, jerking away from her grasp and sinking back into the couch.

"I wasn't watching where I was going and ran into someone that was just going about their day as they should," I say; she looks at me as if that weren't enough. I sign in remorse. "I'm late because I went to see Billy," I say admittedly. Brittany is still looking deep into my one good eye as if searching, crawling her way to something truthful. "That's it. I thought he would be there this time," I say tearfully.

"You can't keep doing this, Sam," she says, sitting on the couch beside me; she reaches over and rubs my back. She turns my head to face her. "This isn't healthy," she says softly, and I cry. In the three years we've been married, Brittany had never seen me shed a tear, not even when my father died. Despite how cold he was to my mother, I was very close to that man. Maybe that's the side of the family I get most of my traits. Then again, most of that side of the family is either dead or somewhere in Oregon.

"You can't keep doing this to yourself or your family," she says severely. I nod, agreeing, only to know that wasn't enough, and she wants to continue, but she claps her hands together. "How was your first day of therapy?" she asks almost aggravatingly, picking up the notebook. She is the only person I will emotionally allow to look into the notebook because it's filled with stories of my emotions.

"I will go back to work tomorrow," I say as she turns right to *Yesteryear*. She smiles and looks at me through her eyelashes.

"That's good. I like the title of this one, by the way," I nod in appreciation. I can tell she is trying to change the topic, so I wouldn't get any more upset than I already am, and I love her for that. She looks down at the page. "You haven't even started on it?" I look over at the beer-smeared wall, and the hint of a smile goes through my face. She hands the notebook back. "I'll let you get back to it," she says, smiling. That's the same perfect smile I love so dearly. I thank her and take out my pen, beginning the workings of a story.

Tuesday: Way back Yesteryear, I was a happy husband but an angry man. Everyone is guilty of feeling the burn of anger once or twice. We all feel this emotion until we taste that beautiful brightness of the liquor named Peaceful. Don't we?

I think back to my time on the train and how the world had felt new, and only then did the world feel different. I felt different. As I finished the sentence, I began to realize this story.

My story will never be told in the land of prying eyes. One can dream; however, can't I? At least, that's what I was led to believe growing up. It's always important to dream of good things. It may become true if you are lucky enough to believe in a falsified reality. The harsh truth of this reality is that no one will know about it, and no one will care once you get a real taste of what reality has in store for you. Reality has a name, and its name is Truth.

I smile, pleased with my work, as I close the notebook. I hear the distant sound of crashing waves. I lay down with my arm draped over Brittany's side. I look over and see the hint of a grin on her tired face. I lay my head on the pillow and slowly drift away from this world and into one of the infinite dreams. I feel a child's finger go up my nose, causing me to sneeze on Alex's hand. "Eww," I hear him and his sister scream as they run back into the kitchen.

"Quite the wake-up call," Brittany says beside me, "later today, we need to remove the bed sheets and replace them with clean ones."

I nod, rubbing my eyes tiredly. "You couldn't have woken me up to warn me?" I say playfully, sitting up, my feet hanging over the bed. I shut my left eye quickly as it screams in pain. She tells me how cute Alex and Sarah were coming into our room, tiptoeing, telling her to keep quiet. I smile lightly. I turn around and kiss her cheek, telling her good morning and getting up to start my morning routine. I go over to my cabinet on the left side of the room and open the top and bottom drawers to get out my underwear and blue jeans. After collecting these things, I walk over to the bed and sit them neatly on the foot of the bed. "I put some Tylenol on the sink, and your coffee is waiting for you in the living room," she says as I walk to our closet. "What do you suggest?" I say, running my finger over the different colored dress shirts.

"Go gray with a dark blue tie," she says, getting up from the mattress. "I'm going to make the kids some breakfast. Do you want something?" she says, standing under the door frame.

"Yes, please," I say as I collect my clothing from the bed and walk into our bathroom. I first opened the sink cabinet, grabbed my shaving cream, and spread it evenly over my beard stubble. I hate how my beard makes me look in the mirror; how I look with a beard reminds me of my father. I turn on the faucet, grab my razor, and cut the stubble to the skin. I hold a rag from our towel rack, rinse off the leftover cream from my chin, and check to see if I have gotten every hair. An unfinished shave looks ridiculous on a man, especially when they are going for a clean shave. I take off my current clothing and turn on the hot water first. I turned the cold to the right only a little, not enough to make a huge difference, but my body could feel it between the follicles of water. I grab another washrag, pour a large portion of my three-in-one shampoo, and wash my hair. I get out of the shower to dry off and put on today's clothing; while buttoning my gray dress shirt, I walk out of the bathroom into our bedroom to check the time. There is at least half an hour in between when I have to drop Brittany off at the general store (she is working with a handsome fellow named Marty today, I don't care much for Marty or his pompous eagle tattoo) and when I drop the kids off at the elementary school, leaving the perfect amount of time for me to fill up the Chevy parked beside our house and go to work. I grab my phone, wallet, and, most importantly, the notebook and walk down the hallway.

"I made you some eggs and bacon," Brittany says from the kitchen as I walk into the living room, fixing my hair how I like it.

"I already put it on the table next to Alex's plate," Brittany says as I walk into the dining room and see both plates are empty except for Sarah's. Which has only a tiny amount of eggs inside the platter. I look back into the living room and notice that both kids are watching Looney Tunes (In this week's episode, Bugs Bunny takes Roadrunner's place in Wiley Coyotes' fiendish plans). I never enjoyed cartoons as a kid; I always believed I was too old for all that kiddy paraphernalia. But, in a way, I was. I sit in the chair facing the window and see neighbors across the street walk their children to their cars. Brittany always insisted on gaining new friends in this neighborhood, more than likely trying to get my mind off what happened to Billy. I remember looking over at his bloodied face as we hung upside down in his old truck (the one behind his house). We had run into a semi-truck, rendering my longtime friend to his death. We both died that night. Way back Yesteryear. I finish my breakfast and tell everybody to load up in the car. We dropped the kids off first and sat silently in the general store parking lot for what seemed like hours.

"Are you okay today? I guess you don't seem all there," Brittany says, looking over at me. "You know you can just call out, and they would have a substitute ready," she says reassuringly. I look at myself in the top rearview mirror as if searching for something no longer there.

"I don't know. It just feels strange, like it's all for nothing," I say as a drop of rain falls dead center on the front window, and another droplet follows. "I'm glad to be returning to work, at least I think I am. Suppose I don't know what to feel anymore," I say, eyeing the red truck parked beside a lamppost (the bulb had long been broken). I'm relatively sure that it is Marty's truck. I decide against myself and don't bring up the question. No matter how much I want to.

"Well, if you feel like heading home early, there is no shame in that," Brittany says enthusiastically as she kisses my cheek and exits the car. I smiled out the corner of my mouth, turned on the ignition, put the vehicle in drive, and made my way to work.

CHAPTER THREE

Ï parked the van across the street from the school in front of a discount
clothing store called The Perfect Fit. I knew the owner from high
school; it was the only reason Mary Dinway passed her math ACT. That
part of my life is now almost long since forgotten. I wonder if she
remembers my name. I leave the car with my notebook and look in the
store window to see if she is working. She is not, but I was greeted with a
fake smile and a half-haphazard wave. I do the same back and make my
way into the school building. The breakfast bell rings, and a few students
are behind in entering the building but not late enough to be considered
delinquent. Our student levels have dropped over the past two years, it's
pretty sad to see, yet little over one hundred students still have the burning
desire to make something of themselves. I wave and hug my coworkers
quickly as I enter the office to see the superintendent and the principal. I
chuckle as I hear the loud pops as my dress shoes crash on the neatly tiled
flooring. At this moment, I am in a state of euphoria. I have finally made
it home. I continue to carry my smile as I walk into the office, the dark
blue shag carpet scratching against my shoes, causing a pleasant ripple to
go through my ear cases. Enthused, I walk over to the desk of Mrs. Carrie,
whom I never made the time to learn her last name, even if she has been
doing this job far longer than I ever have. I could buy the yearbook for

this year, but I see that is pointless, especially after this year she is set for retirement; a shame. I enjoy her quick wit and snarky remarks.

"Hello, Carrie, you look lovely as ever, are Victor and Casey in the office?" I asked.

"Yes, they are ready and waiting for you," she answers while checking her phone. I nod, placing my notebook on her desk. That's another thing I liked about Carrie. She didn't get involved in my business "your back amongst the living, Mr. Dark?" she says under her breath, taking the notebook and placing it under her keyboard. I could drop dead any second if the time has anything to say about it. I answer to myself, trying to think of better thoughts, but none come to mind. I can't go in there feeling like this; they might suspend me permanently. I open the door as those thoughts continuously race around the never-ending track of the human mind leaving nothing behind besides the walls of sudden thought and the ramps of the past. I open the door keeping my eyes on the ground, timid and afraid of what they might say. This office was the only one to change significantly over the summer. Victor (The principal) now has photographs of his newborn daughter and his wife, they seem happy in those pictures, and I'm glad for him. He owns a Georgia O'Keeffe painting, a bright mixture of blues, blacks, and grays. I study this painting for a longing moment to feel its presence in the room. I look over to Victor.

"Is that an original?" I hear the slight pig noise come from the superintendent. Victor shakes his head. "I didn't think so," I say, giving them both a faint smile as I go over and sit. We didn't speak until the Superintendent entered the room; she had a calming aura that I couldn't quite explain. I just wanted to feel better when she was near. I'm sure the other two felt this way as well. I had hoped they did. Hoping they did help me feel less alone than in Yesteryear. Of course, the help doesn't last long, but the thought is what matters.

"Your, Mr. Dark, I presume. I'm the new superintendent Casey" she says, reaching out to shake my hand; I take it reluctantly. "So, considering recent events, we have concluded as to how you will spend the remainder of the school year here" shocked, I let go of her hand and turned to Victor.

"You had the meeting without me" I suppose he could feel my frustration; who wouldn't be if their boss suddenly decided something without the person in question's input? He tells me they had no choice in the matter, considering my returning to work so early on is never the healthiest decision. "I'm sorry, Victor, but that's complete bullshit!" he tells me to calm down and listen to this woman's words. "So what does that mean for my teaching?" I ask, looking into her hazel eyes with the slightest anger. I know she can feel its burn through my eyes. I sense she is laughing on the inside, and I hate that. Right now, I hate just about everything. I wish I could just run away and get this over with.

"Your teachings will go on accordingly, but for the remainder of this year, you are to report to me if you are prepared mentally and up to all the tasks a teacher requires." She says as if she has something better to do with her time. This is a waste of my time. I should be in that room teaching, not some substitute who probably knows less than nothing about psychology.

"I already have a therapist to talk about my feelings to, and I don't need another one," I say, looking at her surprisingly in remorse. Darkness is hidden behind those eyes and that smile; I hold back a grin. That is going into the notebook, I think to myself.

"If you want to keep your job Mr. Dark, you will report back to me!" She says in a slight teenage angst sort of way. The kind in movies where the teenager gets angered because they can't go out and see their high school sweetheart who, unbeknownst to them, is cheating on them with what we, the watcher, are led to believe to be the only attractive person who goes to the school. Of course, this does not often happen in reality, but movies tend to bring about more drama than they should in their stories.

"All right, but I'm not going to come down here every time that bell decides to sing," I retort.

"Fine, just make sure you report to me," she agrees, saying she is pleased we have understood one another. I agree with this and step out of the office and retrieve the notebook. On my way down the hallway, I stopped by the employee restroom and splashed water onto my face, causing my dress shirt's neck to grow cold and damp. I look into the mirror and can no longer recognize myself. Dark circles rest at the bottom of my eyes, and my face has grown pale. I fix my hair with my wetted hand, matting it against my forehead. I check the hallway and see no one coming up or down. I lock the door, return to the mirror, and take a disappointing look into my soul. Worthless, I think as I ball my left hand into a fist, and my knuckles grow white.

"Fuck!" I screamed, punching the mirror with all my force and hatred. I stand there for a long time, letting the warmth of my blood wash over my hand into the sink. Finally, I take my fist out of what used to be a very nice mirror and look at my knuckles seeing minor cuts; they weren't deep enough to cause any of the glass shards to stay in my hand but sufficient to generate questioning from Brittany. I run my good hand over the paper towel dispenser sensor and wrap the paper towel tightly around the cuts on the knuckles. Hopefully, they won't ask, I think to myself as I tie a knot on the palm of my hand and squeeze it tightly as I open the door and stroll down the hallway. I walk into a classroom full of chatter and half the empty seats. "Fill up the rows, please!" I say, walking to the chalkboard and writing Mr. Dark in big, bold red lettering. They do as I ask without question filling up the empty seats to the left of the room. I will have them use the other chairs for future group assignments, I think to myself. I turn around and wait for them to quiet down. Silence, the ringing of tinnitus, fills the empty void.

"I am Mr. Dark; over the past few days, you all have been doing nothing, considering I have been indisposed. So my substitute, Mr. Harvey, will no longer be teaching you what kind of bait to use when fishing," I hear scuffled laughter. "I am much different from Harvey; you are to take my lessons seriously in my classroom. Do you know why I require this?" I say, waving my hands in the air. "Psychology isn't just the study of the mind. Still, it also is the study of the soul." I erase what's on the board, write *Lesson 1* with the same chalk, and turn around. "Might need some paper," I say. Shortly after hearing the clattering and screaming of papers being flipped, "The first lesson of this week will be on human behavior," I turn back to the classroom and see a hand raised. "Yes," I say, pointing to the same girl that read my notebook; she is wearing a green coat and a red T-shirt but still has her pink headband. I can tell it's the same girl. I know it is.

"What happened to your hand?" she asks—that dreaded question.

"And you are?" I remind myself to check the attendance, although I don't see any reason to. Whoever is in this classroom standing before me is all I will ever receive when having a whole classroom. "Nancy?" she nods lightly. I smile, thinking to myself how fitting of a name that is. "I punched something hard," I say, causing some students to laugh. "All right, jumping back to the lesson. I have an assignment for all of you. You are to write half to a multiple-page paper about yourself by tomorrow, and we will talk about what you have written. Simple enough?" I get no answer. "That was a question for the classroom to answer," they answered this time. "Good, get started. When done, put your head on your desk." They take their pencils out of their bags, and I sit. I study them as they write, a boy named Trey seems a bit nervous, and there are other boys in the back being rowdy as teenagers are. I hear my name whispered along with one word, "Freaky" ignoring this, I open my notebook and begin to write myself. I remember the fake smile on the guidance counselor, Billy's realization of self-worth, the phone call on the train, and my own experience with this classroom.

Wednesday: Way back Yesteryear, a person's value was determined by a mere false smile, a mask twisting and shoving down what they feel. I, unlike others, had grown very tired of this mask and its loose strings when I tied it on in the mornings of Yesteryear. Unfortunately, I see others with this same false smile in Yesteryear. They call me a freak simply because I no longer wish to wear this vile mask. I often watch the world pass by as I sit inside a train, watching as the new gray world passes by, leaving behind broken homes and lost dreams in its wake. I sit here stuck in Yesteryear as if I am a statue on a train going nowhere but always somehow reaching its destination. But there is a bright side to this; I am always greeted with the same false smile. That smile holds back deep dark secrets. Way back Yesteryear.

I close the notebook and see five students have finished in the first five minutes of class. "The ones that have finished the assignment early can go out into the commencement area and wait till break" three of the students stand up and turn in their papers. One of them says something under their breath that I can't quite discern. Ignoring this, I turn back to the classroom as the door slams, locking itself into place. Nancy raises her hand high above her head. "Yes, Nancy," I say, moving from my chair and walking over to her desk overlooking her halfway-finished paper. "What's the problem?" She looks up at me.

"You know they just wanted to get out of here early, don't you?" she says, almost as if to ensure I am all there. If she were to ask that, I would simply tell the girl that I have no clue anymore. No one seems to be answering when she knocks on the door. I agree to this and ask her to finish her work; I go back behind the desk and lean back in my chair, watching as the clock seems to go by slower. I close my eyes. My world turns upside down. The front window of that old red truck is smoldered by the blood that does not appear to be mine. I unbuckle my seat belt, and my body twists into a disjointed capital C shape; the airbags had failed us that night. I looked over to Billy, whose head had been caved in by the steering wheel, his cold dead eyes looking deep into my soul. Fearfully I start banging on my door, screaming for help. But no one came until an hour later when I saw flashing red and blue lights somewhere behind the hill of the road and the sounds of the school bell ringing. I dismissed the classroom reminding them that the assignment was due tomorrow morning. They all acknowledge this by making their way down the hall.

"Have a good rest of your day Mr. Dark?" Nancy says, making her way up the row. I lean forward, quickly hide the notebook, and get out my attendance sheet. I will never see most students missing today in this classroom, so I mark them absent for the remainder of the week. I have no first- or second-year students in my itinerary; they are just upper-level students.

"Good is a word we never use in this classroom," I say under my breath; she stops cold in the middle of her stride.

"Why not?" she asks. Nancy brought so much heart into one question that it almost caught me off guard.

"Good is nothing but a word to describe someone's fantasy. Sure, it's considered a feeling and is loosely based on the purity of emotion, which is also the brain's way of telling the rest of the body a little white lie. Yes, we are studying why people feel the way they do and why we act the way we do. We all have a story we like to tell ourselves. Hidden behind that story is neither an emotion nor fantasy. It's the truth." She stares into my eyes as if astonished by my claims. She starts to rub her left shoulder. She's nervous, I think to myself.

"What's your truth Mr. Dark?" she asks timidly. I rock back in my chair, reminded of Billy's bloodied face.

"I have no clue," I say not only to her but also to myself. I check the time and leave the classroom, leaving Nancy alone to her thoughts. I walked into the front office and asked if they could send a substitute for the rest of their day. They could. I thank them and quickly run to the car and drive to the bank, almost hitting another car as I pull into the main road. Their car screams as both of our lives could have met their end. "You're not that lucky," I tell myself, parking on the corner of the building. I park the car, go over to the pay phone, pay the twenty-five cents, dial the number to the HMT (Helpful Minds Therapy) phone number, and wait for someone on the other line to pick up. "Hello, HMT support speaking," the voice matched the young woman from yesterday.

"Hello, my name is Samuel Dark. I came in yesterday," she recognized my vote instantly. "I was wondering if I could come in early," my voice sounded worrisome. She asked me how early, "as early as I can get," she concurred and put me down for 11:30, which was about half an hour from now. I hung up without thanking her, drove to the general store, parked near the door, and ripped out a piece of paper from the notebook, which has always brought me so much pain. I take out my pen and write in the center of the page. *I need a break.* I put the paper on the dashboard, bring my notebook, and get out, locking the car. I wave to the cashier working and ask if he could watch over the car keys until Brittany arrives. He says he will, and I can tell the boy means it. I bend the notebook and put it in my back pocket. I put my hands deep into the pockets of my jeans and started walking on the side of the road through the overgrown grass. Once inside the meeting room, I sit there, breathing harshly.

"How are you, Sam?" Sharlin says, holding out her hand. I ignore the gesture, go over to the couch, and sit down, breathing heavily. Noticing this, she gets down on her knees and grabs both of my hands wispily, saying, "Slow your breathing," I do as she says, closing my eyes as my heart rate starts to slow. "Good. Now breathe in," I take a longing breath and hold it till I can hear the birds in the trees chirping. I hear the mockingbird sing and let all the air out, opening my eyes. Sweat falls from my temple onto the floor. What's wrong with this man? I picture this woman saying clearly through those blinking green eyes. "Now tell me what happened," she says, easing me into things. I take a sharp breath and look down.

"I haven't told you much about Billy Freeman, have I?" Smiling. She moves onto the couch across from me and shakes her head. "Billy Freeman was my best friend in college from when friends were a rarity. But there was something about that man I simply could not figure out. Maybe it was a gut feeling telling me I had found someone like me. Broken and afraid," I smile more to myself than the rest of the world. "There was this one time we had gone to a bar together for a big birthday party for one of the more well-known students, the type. The kind of students who wouldn't give two shits about some low-down dirty nobody's like us," I stop to clear my throat. "Anyways, we found a set of twins at this party." I began to laugh hysterically, causing her to laugh. She has a unique laugh that sort of makes her sound as if a goose were shredded apart. "We all got very drunk, me and Billy would transition between each girl because we were too plastered to tell which was mine or his. At the night's end, we would take each other's girl, and do you know what? A few years down the line, Billy married the girl I was supposed to sleep with. I married Brittany, someone I met a year after graduation when I was still deciding what I wanted to do." She looks at me profoundly, admiring the strength and the pure joy I felt while telling that story, which has almost long since been forgotten.

"Tell me about your wife," she says curiously, resting her chin on a closed fist behind the couch cushion "you didn't mention her yesterday during our first session," she says almost remorsefully. I don't deserve it. I know she knows that. I grow uncomfortable and want to crawl back into a little huddle that is only fit for me. I remember doing something similar as a child when the *cool* kids didn't pick me for dodgeball. I never blamed them, and I still don't. Those kids taught me how to bottle up my emotions. We're past that barrier now, or at least we should be. I take out the notebook and place it on the table.

"She isn't perfect. No one is. She tries to be strong and not pushy about how I'm feeling, and I love her for that; I do. But sometimes I wonder if we wouldn't be better off arguing about it. Maybe she would be better off without me as a burden. We never told the kids; their young minds would not begin to fathom the amount of pain I would feel telling them the truth. So I put on a fake smile and pretend everything is all right when I know that's far from the truth. But, then again, what is the truth but a lie?" The room falls deathly silent as I close my eyes, and flashes of that fateful night fly by, all that blood, and none of it was mine? I deserve to die for not trying to help my best friend and not saving my brother in arms. I don't deserve what is given to me.

"Do you ever wonder why you haven't discussed this with Billy's wife?" she says as if that were an option; I couldn't put her through that. I couldn't put myself through that again. "It's true about what you said that no one is perfect; the pursuit of perfection clouds our judgment as humans. You need to talk about this with your wife, even if she isn't, for lack of a better word, pushy on the subject. What do you see as the truth Sam?" she says, looking into me as if full of admiration and wonder. I remember a time when I used to look at things with such curiosity. I hesitate for a moment thinking back to Billy's last letter.

"They will only see me once I'm gone. All that pain and my weaknesses will be held on a pedestal once I'm gone. Even in death, no one knows who you are or where you come from. They never care," I say coldly. She looks at me for a longing moment, perhaps thinking there is no help. Still, she will try. I can respect that dedication to her craft even if it differs vastly from mine. "Can I ask you something?" I say, looking down at the notebook and back to her. Sharlins brows parched as if waiting. "Why are you helping me? Is it because I paid for it or because, unlike most, you care?"

"I'll let you decide," she says admittedly. She taps the notebook cover "are you ready for me to see what you have written? She says, picking it off the table and onto her lap, she looks at me, and I nod. She flips through the first twenty pages, skimming through finished stories until she lands on the one that looks as if recently written. "Yesteryear. I like that," she says half, smiling and reading silently. She closes the notebook silently, looking at the purple covering silently; she looks over at me. "Wow," she says, giving the notebook back to me, "what is the meaning of that term? Yesteryear," I force myself to answer.

"I'm not sure," I say. Sharlin gets up from the couch, goes over to her desk, opens one of the cabinets, takes out a small bottle of blue pills, and hands them to me. "Antidepressants?" I look at the white labeling, turning it over with my fingers.

"I'm going to need you to take two per day for the next week until I get back," she says, writing a note for me to take home. "You can get another prescription when I get back from my business trip," I hesitate to freeze in place.

"Who am I supposed to see while you're gone?" I ask nervously, noticing that I close my eyes, breathing in slowly and exhaling, and my shoulders lose their stiffness. I look back at her. "What am I supposed to do?" I say pleadingly, thinking to myself about how pathetic I am. I fall into a haze as she explains how it's only a week and I should be fine until she returns. How does she know this? She says if I need anyone to talk to, just turn to my wife. I can't because she will be soft on me, and I don't want that. I close my eyes until the end of today's session. I wish her good luck on whatever business venture she is returning to. We shake hands, and I leave the building cradling the notebook between my side and arm. I step on each crack, thinking she is giving up on me; that's the point of the pills. It gives an incentive. I open the bottle, take two glowing blue pills, and continue walking.

CHAPTER FOUR

I t was a short walk out of town and up Vally Hill. I stop to take a few deep breaths and open the gate, which screams in pain from years of being underused. Many don't remember this place, I realize as I walk in through the gate, looking at each stone house in which many now reside; the wind is calm against my face, fallen leaves tumble the way of the wind as it blows, I enjoy the crunch of the leaves, I look both ways before turning down the left road looking at the names on the little houses and stop. We stood there for what seemed to be hours, letting the silence speak for itself. I take out the pill bottle and pop two more into my mouth, tasting the outer wall's sweet texture. The first batch kicked in once I went half a mile from the town. I could tell because I know a symptom of antidepressants is dry throat, not that it matters in hindsight. I tuck the bottle back into my right pocket. I see the trees slowly sway in a dancer-like fashion as if they have something to be proud of. What could that be? I clear my throat and sit down cross-legged on the leaves. I clear the doorstep of its leaves and wipe down the door using my sleeve. I turn the sleeve seeing a long black streak down my forearm. I sigh, looking down at the rows of lifeless houses this time of year and any other year after. We used to come here during high school. I remember vividly all the drinking and tomfoolery we used to get into. I remember once back in Yesteryear, a boy named Trey Rapherdy got so unbelievably drunk he fell into one of these houses, ruining what once was a peaceful slumber; I look around and see the one on the west side still has a caved-in roof. The person who once lived in that house is probably nothing but dust at the bottom of a cement box. I laugh uneasily to myself, remembering how scared we were back then; as children, we had a natural affinity towards things we never understood, ignoring what was in front of us. I look at the door and hear a bird chirping in the distance. It sounds like a hummingbird. I close my eyes. Billy sits beside me as I scream for him to slow down. He denies it. We were in the left lane going seventy-five on a fifty-speed limit freeway in the dead of night; no one else was on the road that night.

No one besides us and the semi-truck barreling down the highway right in front of us. I quickly reached over and turned the wheel at the last second. Unfortunately, the semi-clipped the back of the truck, causing the car to skid down the freeway and suddenly flip over onto its roof. I had made sure my body was limp, and the airbags were broken, leaving Billy lifeless, sitting upside down, drenched in his blood. I unbuckled my seat belt and fell onto the roof, distorted as if I were a typical pretzel. I got out my phone and reported the incident to the best of my ability; my voice was high, and almost too terrified to speak. I remember telling the lifeless body everything would be okay as I opened the door and stumbled onto the road ignoring the broken glass.

The semi was parked a short walk down the road. The driver was running back to check on us. I told the man that my friend was dead, and he patted my back and told me he was sorry as he walked me to a small bed of grass on the side of the road. I remember sitting there for what seemed like hours, drunken, apart from an eternal state of euphoria. I remember not attending the funeral, causing Sandy to despise my family and me. I had always been cold about funerals, so I never cried. I didn't cry when either of my parents died. That must say a lot about me as a person. What do I care? I have no face to these people. I am a faceless husk. I open my eyes and see that everything has remained in place, this cemetery. It's somehow lost in time, neither future nor past, which terrifies me briefly as tears slowly trickle down from their bedspread. I ignore the heavy crackle thinking it must be a foreign animal that made its way through those gates.

I pay attention when I hear hard plastic falling onto the softened ground. I shake my head and wipe away the tears, wishing I were again stuck on that beach. I quickly get up from the dirt and dust off my bottom. I look past one of the houses and see a large bouquet of red roses rising and falling slowly in and out of view. They would be invisible to the naked eye if they stayed in that one spot; like all things, it remains in motion. She is wearing a long black coat, blue jeans, and a green turtleneck; she falls frozen once she sees me. She takes a long breath, passes me by, and lays the flowers on Billy's tomb; she grunts beside me.

"It's been a while, Sam," she says coldly, staring at her husband as if he were standing before her this second. "Thought you would be long gone by now. Knowing what happened, I figured you to be the running type," she says tauntingly. I look over at her and see a long strand of gray in her once beautiful brown locks. We all are getting older with the times changing, some faster than others. I remember Billy telling me once upon a time in Yesteryear. I don't know why I like that word so much when it means nothing in the grand scheme of life.

"I'm not. I've learned to stay simply because I have nowhere to go or anywhere to be. I'm stuck here, Sandy; we're all trapped in a hole with no way out". I say, trying to keep the conversation as point-blank as I can. "How are you dealing with everything?" I ask her. She laughs at the irony of the question, thinking about how all this is somewhat funny.

"Like any grieving woman should. I couldn't stay in that house any longer; too many memories and horrible dreams rest there; I remember seeing you standing at the door. You stopped. I remember wondering if you would hear the music playing. Billy always loved that song, you know." Sandy said coldly; she was trying to keep up the appearance of this ordeal, not fazing her, but I could tell there was a deep love for Billy and a burning hatred for me, which I never blamed her for. "I'm running away, Sam," she says, looking deep into my eyes.

"Where will you go?" I asked solemnly. Sandy hesitates before answering the question as if she hasn't planned to go anywhere.

"I don't know, maybe past the trees and the meadows, I will run to paradise," she stops and thinks briefly. "I'll be free. Billy was right, you know. This world is falling apart sooner than we would like it to. There isn't a way to stop it from happening. The kids have moved on now. To someone more equipped to care for them," she starts crying. I inch myself over and put my arm around her shoulder. "How I miss them so. They are the only reason I have remained in this world. I don't know why I am staying now. They have forgotten all about little old me," she says, laughing amongst herself as I stare off into the distance.

"Maybe. Maybe this world is coming to an end, and so are we. That's the breaking-off point, I believe. When your child no longer sees you for who they know you by. The one that will always be there to catch them when they fall. Now they have found someone new. Maybe that's a good thing," I say; she wipes away a ball of mucus.

"Why do you always have to be so dry," she says, and we both laugh, the kind of laugh when you feel uncomfortable because you have said something wrong in the middle of a party.

"I never blamed you for his death," she whispers.

"I do. Everyday. I constantly have to fight the urge to end it all because of my family," I say, surprised. As of late, I have been more open with people, and I can't decide if that is good or bad. In the end, it doesn't matter, I think to myself. She lets out a loud laugh.

"Welcome to my world Sam, except in mine; I no longer have anything to live for but you. You have a family; you're supposed to be the one that has it all figured out. The big shot writer! Not too good for those big city wigs and not too bad for us down here on the ground level. We are all supposed to be fucked up, yet you are sulking. You're supposed to be the best of us, Sam." She whispers as her voice rises and falls, not only for me but for Billy to hear as well as he rests at the bottom of his tomb. I lift my arm from her shoulder and turn to leave.

"Not anymore, it would seem. I'm sorry for what happened with Billy; I truly am Sandy. I hope you find your reason to continue with your life." I say, walking away.

"That reason is at the bottom of a box," I hear her say as I walk past her black Honda accord and down the hill. I jump, hear the gunshot blow from the top of the mountain, and close my eyes. I don't bother to turn back. I continue to walk down the long road and into town. I stopped by the general store and saw that the van was missing. I curse under my breath and take two more pills that don't take effect until I reach about a half mile from the main road to our house. Finally, I decided to jog the rest of the way. I lift the flowerpot at the bottom of the stair, open the door, and tiptoe into our room. I don't care to notice that the car is no longer parked in the driveway or the note on the fridge; I limp, fainting in and out of reality. I lay on the soft mattress, slowly fading into a deep slumber. I am placed in the cemetery again; the world is gray and colder than usual.

For some ungodly reason, I look down at my feet and see the corpse of Sandy; a large hole was burned into the side of her head, clouding her permanently smiling grin in blood, finally giving it some color. Billy's tombstone is located on the far end of the cemetery, his voice telling me in a whisper in the wind. "You could have saved me," I look away and see Sandy repeating the singer's words. "You could have saved me," I shake my head and run towards the gates and bash my shoulder through opening them. A mirror stands in front of the double-sided gates, and an aberration of I appears without a face. I reach out to this mirror, which shatters at the bottom of the tip of my shoe. I awaken in a sweaty heap, falling onto the floor tangled in the bedspread.

I get off the floor, letting the blanket lie there as I walk into the kitchen, take out the bottle of pills, and stumble, grabbing the refrigerator door and opening it, and grabbing a leftover sandwich and a Diet Fizz. I tap the top before opening it and take both of the pills.

I look over to check the time and see it is five in the morning. I close the door and see the yellow sticky note: *Call if you need to talk. I'm going to Wilma's with the kids.* I rush to the home phone and call the number left at the bottom of the note. It rings for hours, and her sister picks it up. Her sister is nice enough but a bit of a bore to talk to most of the time.

"Hello?" she says into the speaker.

"Hey, Will, do you mind putting Britany on the phone, please?" She does as I say without any sense of hesitation. Brittany must be near the phone, considering it doesn't take long for her to rest it on her shoulder.

"Hey," she says quickly.

"Hi," I say back. "I wanted to say I'm sorry," I say, walking into the living room and turning on the News. They were covering suicide in a local cemetery.

"What for?" she asks.

"Just a second," I say, putting the phone back on the couch. Then, I turn off the television, return to the room, and grab my notebook and pin. Then, quickly walk back into the living room and grab the phone. "I'm sorry for not calling you any sooner," Brittany sighs into the phone.

"What's going on, Sam?" she asks hesitantly.

"I don't know, Brit. Maybe I'm stuck like this. The therapist has given up on me; she gave me a thing of pills today. Antidepressants that don't work a damned bit," I say, throwing the bottle into the trash. "There is one thing I know for sure. I can't have you give up on me too. If you do that, I might not be here when you return," I say. We fall into an empty silence that not even a modern field mouse could mask with the clatter of its little feet.

"What do you want me to do, Sam? I can't be in the same house as you. It makes me sad to see you like this. There is only so much I can take," she takes the phone into the living room, and I can hear her flop down on the couch.

"I want you here in case I get lost again," I say. Brittany hesitates and hangs up the phone; I do the same and lie down on the couch and fall back asleep. I wake up to the phone ringing, feeling the space where Brittney was always comfortable and answering with a haphazard grunt as I get up and walk into the kitchen and take a gray bowl and a spoon out of their separate cabinets and make some cereal. Before reaching up to grab two more, I remember there is no one else in this lonesome house except me and what I would like to call the feelings of Yesteryear. Victor was on the other end, asking me if I could return to work. I agree, finishing my bowl and rinsing it out. I walk back to our bedroom and prepare for the day in the same style as yesterday, except I decide to wear my dark blue coat. With my notebook in hand, I walked to the nearest bus stop and sat beside an older woman who seemed to be having it rough; then again, it was all rough these days.

I lean over, as curious as ever as to why? Why such curiosity? Why now? "Are you all right, ma'am?" She looks around, shakes her head, and tells me how her oldest son died earlier today from a stroke. I gave my condolences and helped her onto the bus, and we talked until the bus stopped in front of a nursing home. A woman wearing her uniform was standing there as if she were a statue with a big fake smile forever welded into that mask of hers. I wave at the elder as the bus moves forward, wishing her luck in silence. We all need a bit of luck in the coming days, I think to myself as I relax into the seat. I pay the fee, get off the bus and walk into the school building. The Superintendent asks me how I am doing today. I answer with a thumbs up, unlock the door to my classroom, and open my notebook. Once I press the ink onto the paper, the door opens, and I am interrupted by Nancy coming in through the door and waving at me. She quickly lays the report on my desk and goes to take her seat; I take the time to notice that the whole class is five minutes late. You've got to keep up appearances, I think to myself, taking the paper titled *Pink* and beginning to read.

Pink

By: Nancy W.

In a day or two, I will be sitting in the same position as today, wondering if the conclusion of this world will come. I will have nothing to do but wait for the call of my name coming from the top of the summit, where we all shall plummet into the sea of eternity. On that day I will finally wear Pink. A beautiful mixture of love and purity creates what I would like to call hope. I will always have hope somewhere near the time the final sunset comes about. Others will share this hope because, in the end, that's all we will have. Some will not share this hope and will not reach the summit, but they will wait. They will wait for the reason they came and find none. I am hopeful that we will all learn to see the color pink in the end.

"Why?" I ask. She looks up from her desk.

"Excuse me?" she says, coming up to my desk.

I get up and go around and take a random chair from under a table and place it in front of my desk; I motion for her to take a seat, and in slight hesitation, she does so. I walk around the desk and plop down into the chair, unbeknownst to my notebook being wide open for the world to see.

"In this story, you describe yourself as hopeful, correct?" she agrees. "Why do you feel such hope for a world gone to shambles, born from the decrepitation of war?" But, I ask her, even if this is partly true, I am more than willing to hear from the second point of view. Sometimes that can change the entirety of how we see the world. She breathes in deeply as if anxious. She has never done something like this before. Interesting, I think to myself.

"Do you not?" she asks hesitantly; surprised at the longevity of the question, I rock back on the table. "I'm not sure as to how I feel anymore. It's all going to end the same, with all of us counting the rose petals that fall from their stems when they were six feet under a large bed of dirt. So, no, I don't feel such hope," I say admittedly. She begins rubbing her left shoulder.

"It sort of sounds like you are searching for something," her voice mere inches away from being a whisper. I let out a longing breath.

"We all are searching for something, Mrs. Nancy. You are searching for something we are told from birth to believe in, and I respect that highly but what you're looking for has come to a bare minimum. No one has hope anymore, not for themselves nor the world around them," I say, leaning towards her.

"I know. That's why we need all we can get from what we have," Nancy says as she starts for her seat. "Can I ask you something, Mr. Dark?" I nod in agreement. "What are you searching for?" I go to answer when the door opens, and a sea of ten students comes through. I get off the table and go behind the desk, and they all take their seats.

"Welcome. How was everyone's morning?" I say, flashing my fake grin as I place the seat back into its original position. Hopefully, someone back there can see through the lie. They all say they're doing fine, which is a lie, and I can tell. "All right, the first rule of my classroom, you come in late, you stay late, so that means all of you that was!" I check the clock above the blackboard. "Eighteen minutes late, which means you all will have to deal with me a few more minutes before you all go about your day," they groan. "This is your wrongdoing, and it is your responsibility to fix this. So now everyone gets out your papers from yesterday, and the class will begin," they all do so with angry expressions painted on their canvas.

What do I care? Their anger won't change anything. They all walked up to the desk and turned in their papers; all were much more grounded and true to the mind of a prepubescent teenager. I grab the documents, quickly skim through them, place them back in the open notebook, and turn back to the class. "Congratulations, all of you, for turning in your first quiz grade. What do you all say to me reading some of these?" Quite a few moan and groan as if they were still children who are all simultaneously complaining about their stomachs hurting so they can get out of going to school for the week. I take the paper on top of the stack written by Trey Edgerton, or as some would call him, Top, and read.

"This is from mister Top in the back there," I take a deep breath and make my voice as high-pitched as possible. "This motha' fucker really think we gonna do dis?" They all laugh. "Under that, we have a response from Mike Edgerton," I begin to smile at the incorrect spelling. "Yeh, this is really dumb," I laughed slightly. "Thank you both for your riveting input. I will remember it once I do more projects such as this one. The rest of you, what do you think should be the grade for this paper? I'm thinking an F minus; neither of you showed any effort in this assignment, which will affect the rest of this classroom's grading for the remainder of the year." I hear someone complain about this not being fair. "It's not fair that I have to deal with such a lack of effort or grit to finish things properly. I am very aware that this is our first assignment. Well, guess what? I don't care what it is. I want you all to give me one hundred percent on each assignment from here on out. Do we have an understanding?" They all nod, and I go back behind the desk. "Good. Trey and Mike get up here and pass these papers back out," they both do as I say and pass the papers to their original owners. "Now that you all have your papers back,

I want to do a little experiment. Pass the papers around until I tell you to stop," they all do so. I wait a few more moments, walking around the desk and checking if anyone has kept their papers.

"Stop," they halt; once I am pleased with the outcome, I return to the desk and sit on the edge. "All right, now we are going from the left of the room to the right until we finish off the day with Trey back there in the corner. All right, Missy Winters, please read your paper so the class can hear," I say, folding my arms. She is very timid and can almost not finish the first three sentences. The second boy has a speech impediment causing his sentences to jumble together, which I can't blame him for. I, too, had a speech impediment for the better half of my middle school year, which caused me to get bullied exclusively by this big Spanish boy named Hosea Martinez. I wonder if this boy gets bullied much, which would seem redundant. The rest of the stories were below my standards, but no one was perfect. That is one thing I must remember for the remainder of the year. These kids. They are much more emotional than most adults, and maybe that's a good thing. It keeps them tethered to the ones they love. I look down at my shoes and think back to Brittany. The one person who understands me is staying away from me. There is some sadness in this thought, but I decided against showing it. Knowing these children, they would laugh and frolic at their teacher crying in the middle of class.

"All right, I think it is time to discuss. What have we learned about the person we just read from?" I say with another false smile; I think back to Yesteryear and how much this story untold will change anything. Probably nothing. In the end, it will solve nothing. There is no reason for Yesteryear which means there is no longer reason to continue. No, there must be a reason behind why Sharlin gave me Yesteryear. Why would she have so much trouble getting me to feel better? There has to be more to it. There has to be justification. Right?

CHAPTER FIVE

Thursday: Way back Yesteryear, I was a happy husband but an angry man. Oh, so very angry. There was no rational reason for this anger, was there? No, there is no reason for outrage in this world, nor is there a reason for anything. I met another faceless person today. For the oddest reasons, she has found her justification to stay in Yesteryear while I still search for my own. I found it amusing once I found out her name, and it is not only associated with color but also the color of love and hope. Pink. That was her name once upon a time in Yesteryear.

Nothing. I still find nothing, and I feel nothing. Once I finish the sentence, I scratch out the sentence and rewrite it. Come on, I tell myself—still nothing. I rip out the paper from the notebook causing it to scream in pain as I shred the pieces and let them fall slowly into the floor. I look around and notice the empty school, and I will have to leave soon. I repeatedly rewrite, replacing each word and symbol and waiting to feel anything. After a while, I give up, letting the ink from the pen drip down, leaving large black stains on the paper. The world falls cold and silent as I close my eyes and imagine the beach that remains a mystery. What is this place? I ask myself, hoping for an answer—hope, what a feeling it must be. Finally, someone knocks on the door. I motion for them to come in as I look down at the large black blotch overtaking what is already written.

This person ushers forward and stands there until I grow uncomfortable with their presence. I look up and see that it is Nancy. I flash my false smile.

"How can I help you this fine evening, Miss Nancy?" I ask, looking out the window and seeing the waterfall of rain overflowing my sight into the outside world; I laugh at the irony.

"How did you become such a bitter man? A sad man who hides behind a smile whenever he comes in here? I know you have only been here twice, but I assure you that not everything is as bad as you seem to think," she says tearfully. She almost sounds as if she is remorseful, and I can admire that.

"I don't know. I can't tell you that more recent events caused it because that would be lying, which I have grown into a master of, but with you, Nancy, I won't lie. You deserve the truth because I can tell you are a very hard-working girl, and I admire that. I'll be the first to tell you I'm unsure how to feel about anything. Maybe I never did. Maybe this is the truth behind the mask you see when you walk into class these next few months that we have. I don't know, Nancy. I don't know what I'm looking for. Maybe I'm looking for Yesteryear and why she would lie for so long," I say, looking outside as the world seems inevitable through that hazy gray glass. I look around and see that the walls have gone gray. "My wife doesn't want anything to do with me now. Isn't that a kicker?" I say, leaning back into the chair. "Hope may be the only water we have left to drink from, and I promise that water. It's about to run dry. My pawn has. I drank too much for my own good," I say whisperingly.

"I wish there was an easy way to find what you want. But, maybe you just need to keep looking," she says as if suggesting a board meeting. She has this way about her words, making me think everything coming out is true. Maybe there is some amount of hope left. But how much more?

How much longer am I willing to continue this search? I am afraid I no longer care.

"There is no easy way to find anything in this life, especially hope. There is no reason to. Ultimately, we all will come to oblivion, and none of this will matter. There is a time when you and I are forgotten, as will the rest of us. I'll give you some advice for when you're older. No one cares about your dreams, hopes, or aspirations; we like to think we make a difference here, but we don't. So get with the program, sister, 'cause you have a lot to learn about what life has to offer, and that is despair." she rushes out of the room and down the hall. Maybe you were too harsh on the girl, I tell myself as I close the notebook, put it in my back pocket, and prepare my things. I stroll down the halls, taking in the vast silence surrounding me, perfection. Chasing after is pointless, yet we all find some reason to search. I wait as I stand before the double doors and look down the hallway, and slowly look down the right. I walk down the steps in a light brisk and break out into a jog until I reach a few feet from the local hotel and walk around back. There is a short road that goes down a little way until it comes to an ending reaching the bottom molded over steps. The house looks much older now than when it used to. Its old lime green shutters are a deep dark green that, without a second glance, you would assume were black. I walk down and look at the grass, which is now dead except for small patches. I quickly look in the garage and see our van parked under a loosely built roof with holes punctured through, giving a broken mirror appearance to the sky above. The thought of this grows more beautiful as seconds pass by. I walk up the steps and knock on the door three times. I hear footsteps and Wilmas' voice calling from upstairs, telling me she would be down in a minute. Brittany must be sleeping.

I figure as I look around and see a tall dead tree towering over what used to be a red roof. Anything else this place would turn into a junkie's hang out. The door opens, and Wilma stands there wearing a green face mask and looks as if she has just woken up; she looks up at me with a cold gaze. "How are you getting on, Sammy?" she asks, stepping out onto the porch and sitting on the rocking chair to the left of the door. I always hated the way Will called me that. There is nothing wrong with the name itself. It's the way she says it that bothers me, Will says it as if it were a privilege for me to hear it, making it sound like she has other things to do than say a name. I manage to bring forth another falsified smile. She takes out a pack of cigarettes, takes one out, and covers the flame as it ignites onto the tip of the bud. She takes another out and hands it to me; I wave it off. She chuckles, stuffs it back into the box, and places it underneath her crotch. "Are you gonna stand there like a fucking statue all day, or will you take a seat?" I shrug and take the rocking chair beside her, taking the notebook out, sitting it on my lap, and pressing my fingers down onto the wooden armrest. "What are you doing here, Sammy?" she says again, using that snarky tone.

"I need her back, Wilma," I answer wholeheartedly, looking out past the driveway and seeing the graffiti painted on the backside of the hotel, which is now going into its third consecutive year of being built and already has the words, Rock, Wake Up, and a complete sentence written in sharpie that says. *"We hide our feelings, but we forget that our eyes speak"* this is true for most, but the rest have grown to be masters of putting on that vile mask, the one with the false smile and the pleading eyes. "I need them back," I say full-hearted.

"That's the problem. You need Brittany and the kids more than they need you. I know how you are, you're going through some tough shit, but I have to ask when it will end? When will you learn to stop and take into consideration the well-being of others? It hurts her to see you like this. She told me you have had these feelings on a lower scale since you met. Now she thinks you've gotten worse; that's why she left. She didn't want to see what would happen if you; hurt yourself or at least try to hurt yourself," she says, looking as if she were looking for an answer; Wilma raises her eyebrows. "Can you at least tell me what is going on here?" she asks almost sarcastically, which causes me to despise this conversation even more. I look at the bright blue sky, watching the clouds slowly crawl by as I look back at her. Wilma's face was pale underneath all that green sludge and bright blue eyes.

"I'm hurting Wilma, I'm hurting real bad. I've been to therapy repeatedly, which doesn't seem to be helping; before Brittany, I went to a psychiatrist and found out I have chronic depression. Ain't that just a little bit funny? I lived my whole life feeling like all this was meaningless, which it is. There is no reason to continue if we're all going to die anyways. There is no point," I say, looking down at my shoes. "Yeah, it has gotten worse. I never cried during funerals, not even the ones for my parents. I didn't cry at Billy's either, and I hate myself for that," I say, admittedly in defeat.

"I'm sorry, I didn't know that, Samuel," she says. I hear tiny footsteps in the living room. It must be the kids, I think to myself; what would I give to see one more smile on their faces? I would give everything, even Yesteryear. I smile.

"You know, I think that was the first time you used my actual name," I say, getting out of the chair.

"What's in the notebook?" She says, taking a long puff out of her cigarette. "You always carry one with you, and I was always curious about what you have in that thing," she says, pointing at the notebook in my hand. I look at the notebook's cover, fold the booklet in half, and put it into my back pocket.

"Yesteryear," I say quietly enough to where she cannot hear. "Deliver a message for me. Tell them I love them, and I'll see them soon" she throws up her arms in defeat.

"Fine, don't tell me what you write. I will. I hope you find whatever you are looking for, Sam," she says. I nod respectfully. I walk down the stairs, back into town, and stop by the general store. The young cashier greets me as I grab a budgie, walk down the office utensil aisle, and grab a notebook with a gray covering over seventy pages in this small booklet. I hold a pack of pens carrying twenty ballpoints and put both in the budgie. I look down the aisle and see Billy standing, his red shirt is dark from all the blood loss. I see Sandy standing on the opposite end, gun in hand. Half the side of her head looks as if it had been blasted off, leaving behind a small pool of brain matter on the checkered tiled flooring, the gun itself pointed dead center on the middle of my forehead. I close my eyes tightly and wait a moment to open them again. Once I do so, I am brought back to the classroom in which everything is colored gray and black. The desk was empty. I looked around the classroom walls and finally noticed the five mirrors on the back wall that revealed nothing. I looked back down and saw all the seats were filled with faceless people except for the one where Nancy chose to sit; I walked over to the desk and found her pink hair band bloodied, both colors shining brightly against the classroom's cold coloring. I open my eyes and find myself back in the general store. I discard the cart, rush to the restroom, drown my face in cold water, and look at myself in the mirror.

"Fucking useless," I say, looking deep into my two eyes. "Why did you have to make that girl run like that, you selfish prick!?" I scream as I punch the mirror, breaking it and causing my facial features to disfigure. I put my hand deep into my pocket, walked quickly out of the rest room and pulled the shopping cart back to the front, all together I purchased ten dollars' worth of two things. I put down an extra twenty dollar bill and told them to spend it on a new mirror for the restroom and walk out of the store and continue down the street. It was nightfall before I reached the house, the orange street lights highlighting my path until I got to our driveway. I unlock the door, turn on the living room lights, and check the time. It is twelve-fifty, I realize as I throw my items in the living room and make my way into the kitchen placing the notebook on the counter. I grab a bowl from the above sink cabinet and a fork; I walk over to the fridge, go to the side, and get the see-through box filled halfway with Ramon.

I take out two packs with beef flavoring and quickly crush them both into the bowl, being sure to take out the flavor packets and fill the bowl with water; next, I put it into the microwave for four minutes and wait in the living room and bask in the pure sorrowful silence, in all this quiet I can still hear the pitter patter of my children's footsteps as they run towards the beautiful smell of Brittany's cooking. I look at the time in the microwave, seeing not only thirty seconds have passed. I go over to the notebook and write only two clean and swift words in their universally known meanings: *Goodbye Pink.* I close the notebook again and hear the microwave begin singing its tune. I take out the bowl, sit it on the table, and lightly sprinkle the beef flavoring in a circular motion around it. After I am done, I make sure to grab my fork. In need of it to cool down, I walk back into the kitchen, get a long knife from its holder, and rest the blade against my wrist to keep the edge away from any significant veins. I don't let it cut me too deeply. The pain screams a song as it burns its way up my arm, leaving a stinging sensation to rest at the base of my shoulder. The cut may not be profound, but it is noticeable; the heat of blood slowly trickles down my wrist and onto the last page I worked on earlier, disfiguring its writing. Kind of fitting, I think to myself as I wrap it in paper towels and go back to the table to finish eating my meal in silence as the blood slowly overflows and drips onto the table; I wash up the plate before going to our bathroom and check the cabinet underneath the sink and take out a see-through box with a blue lid and sit it on the toilet head, I go back into the kitchen and open one of our plastic drawers and take out a zip lock bag, I turn the sink to hot and wait for the bag to fill and get down a white hard plastic bowl and take them both into the bathroom. I wash my hands, remove the mid-shift bandage and let the blood fall into the hot water I poured into the white bowl. I open the underneath cabinet and take out a large bottle of alcohol and pour it onto the wound biting my tongue as the liquid burns its way down the cut. I put my wrist in the water, take out a needle and thread out of the box and thread the hand easily, poke a few inches away from the cut at an angle, and begin to sow my skin back together. I put a bandage over the stitching, turn off the bathroom lights, and put all the items back where they belong (except for the dirty bowl, so I put it in the sink), and sit on the couch in the living room, thinking about what I have done.

"Your wife wants nothing to do with you. Sharlin left. Nancy, the one person who helped you there for a minute, has run off. Why? What the hell is wrong with you, Sam? Why do you push people away? That's the million-dollar question," I say to the empty room. I hear the phone go off in the kitchen and go to take it. "Hello," I say.

"Hey Samuel, how are you!?" the woman says, practically screaming down the phone. I take the phone away from my ear. "It's Sharlin, by the way," she says.

"Oh hey, Sharlin, how is your trip?" I ask, trying to change the subject.

"Well, we're almost done here, and I should be home by tomorrow. So how is the story coming along?" Sharlin asks.

I look at the notebook and the bloodied page. "Still being written," I say. "Then again, there isn't much to me or my story," I say with an uncomfortable smile. "I'm doing well, by the way," I say quickly, staring at the cut. "Yeah, those pills you gave me have been making me feel tired as of late," I say, pulling over a chair and sitting down. "Is that a common symptom?" I ask with genuine curiosity.

"Yes, along with other things we can discuss once I return. How is work?" Sharlin asks. I can hear the pitter-patter of her keyboard as she types down my information. I close my eyes, almost seeing that screen as she organizes her information. **Patient: Samuel J. Dark Date: 3- 24-23**

Patient log: Samuel has been experiencing some fatigue (Note: could be from the Cynthide I have him for his treatment of Chronic Depression). He seems to feel the same as our last meeting, except he has become more open to speaking with me, whereas a few days ago, he hardly ever said much of anything. Samuel is also trying to hide something from his loved ones and me. Why?

She stops typing. "How are your wife and kids?" She asks. My face grows hot as my arms shake. I stammer to answer the question, and she starts typing again. *You fucking bitch! You set me up for this.* How could she know about what happened? She couldn't have; she had been gone for the past few days. What should I say? What should I do? There is nothing to do. I am trapped here among the gray, cold world surrounded by smiles and Yesteryear. We are all stuck here now. We all see the truth. What am I thinking? What is my purpose? There is no gold at the end of this rainbow called life, only more woods to get lost, forever a part of this lie we believe in. Why am I thinking this way? What's wrong with me?

"She is doing okay, and so are the kids," I say with such a high level of incompetence it's almost possible to see through. I lower the phone in hopes of her not hearing the scratch against the shirt as it grinds against the base of my chest. Yesteryear save me. Justify me. Give me a reason for this life.

"Well, that's good," she continues to type. I assume she can order using one imposing hand: **Conclusion: Samuel must have had some sort of falling out with his wife, causing not only his condition but also his strong sense of worry to worsen, this sense causing him to eternally**

believe that he is no longer good enough for his family. Henceforth I must research the underlying conditions that he used to ignore, which now have ignited themselves into something more potent and vicious to himself and those around him in his daily life. I must also study his routine since being approved to be a teacher again by the board. He might also have another person he talks to besides me about his conditions which he is aware of, which fascinated me. He is very insightful about his condition, yet he still wishes to hide them from those who are more than willing to help him. Maybe he is no longer searching for help? Perhaps he is looking for the reason behind why he feels this way.

She finishes typing and breathes in deeply as she checks over her work. She makes edits where needed and changes only minor things that professionals would overlook. Like me, she is a perfectionist, forever searching for what is no longer feasible unless she believes there is such a thing as God. She will rest easily in the sea of eternity with him. We talk for several more hours about our both equally separate lives, and yet there are things we find that we have in common, like our taste in music; we both equally share a fascination with Jazz music, and we are both more or less interested in just the instrumentation of the band that's playing. One thing we do not share in this topic is I like the more serine melancholy instrumentation.

In contrast, she likes classic rock music generated mainly from the 80s, which were good years for music and for the people playing that type of music; I have never been into that type of music. I explained to her it was simply too much for the ears for my taste. Sharlin answered this by saying she doesn't care for my type of music; I told her I could respect that, and she said the same for my taste. We tell each other goodbye once the clock strikes noon; I hang up the phone with a bright smile spread across my face and a skip in my step as I walk into the bathroom and shave off what was left of my beard, and walk down the hallway and close my children's bedroom door. They were never scared of the dark or the things that might be waiting for them as they check underneath their beds in the dead of night; when they find that the noise is simply a rat searching for its share of bread crumbs, I close the door and rest my bare hand on the wood imagining them screaming as they hop on each other's bed. I walk into our bedroom and open our closet door and get out the three pillows that lie evenly on the carpeted floor and take them back into the living room and sit them on the couch before moving the glass coffee table and flop the pillow down on top of one another and lie down hoping for the peaceful sleep we all deserve in the end.

CHAPTER SIX

I t was dark when I awoke to the sounds of gale and rain crashing against the outside walls as if I were in a cheeky horror movie. I closed my eyes once again, and a few moments later… I jumped as a tree came crashing through the home's roof, causing a blackout throughout our area. I curse under my breath as I take my raincoat off its hanger and put it on forcibly as I go outside to check on the damage. The tree has a vast base but was almost close to death anyways. Seeing its limbs crawling into the roof did not surprise me; the tree landed above me and Brittany's room. I rushed back into the house, bringing in a trail of water behind me as I ran to our bedroom and checked the roof; a big hole punctured through the ceiling above where we slept. I hastily lifted the mattress out of the bed frame, pushed it in front of the closet door, and quickly moved out of the room as a river of water came crashing through the large hole, causing the ceiling to collapse. Jesus, I think to myself as I try to make my way over the broken pieces of wood, open the top drawer closest to the broken window, and grab two pairs of underwear and pants. I open the second drawer, grab two T-shirts, walk back into the living room, sit them on the couch, and walk into the kitchen to grab an available store bag from the carrier, put the clothes into the bag, and tie it off. I grab my wallet and check the contents. I have fifty dollars and thirty-eight cents, which should be enough to get me a room at the local motel where the grass is dead. The residents are either drunken whores or cracked-out teenagers who sell methamphetamine and seem to think of themselves as untouchable. Like most young folk these days, they are wrong.

I untied the bag, put the notebook and pen in there, and tied it off. I walk into each room and check each roof; only Brittanys and I have seen the damage and walk out into the pouring rain and walk out into town. Nothing but a ghost town, I think to myself as I walk against the wind current as waves of raindrops crash against my body. I can't stop, I tell myself as I search for the neon red motel sign missing the letter O. Still, there is no light in this eternal darkness. None of the eyes could see. I know the area well, but it is challenging without visual cues. Why the hell did you go out into this, you fucking fool? I ask myself as I begin to slip and slide. I stop this by using both my hands to prevent the sliding. I grunt in pain as my hands scrape across the pavement, causing little cuts as the skin of both hands grows old and soft. I continue to walk with one hand in my coat pocket and the other dripping blood as it carries my bag of clothes. I walk a couple more feet before resting at the base of the motel's sign and breath heavily, force my legs to walk a little further to the closed glass door, and read the poster, which reads: **CLOSED FOR MAINTENANCE.**

Maintenance my ass, I tell myself as I nock hard on the glass door and wait for an answer; someone comes rushing out of the back room masked by the dark room and opens the door and says something I can't make out and pushes me inside and sits me down in a lounge chair one could come by at a local market store; I drop the bag onto the floor and listen as small trickles of blood fall from my hands. The man goes to the back room, grabs his flashlight, and shines it onto my face.

"What are you doing in this weather, Samuel?" Thomas Heart is an older gentleman who has always been kind to me when we see each other in town. He would always offer me a taste of his daughter's newest batch of cookies which I would take in respect.

"Tree crashed through my bedroom ceiling," I say, laughing in a light haze, "I thought I'd come down here and ask if you got any rooms available," I said questioningly.

"I'm sorry to hear that, Samuel; are Brittany and the kids all right ?" he asks while going to the back room and bringing back three packs of bandaids and handing them to me. I rip one and place it onto the base of my hand.

"I wouldn't know. I haven't seen Brittany or the kids for about three days now, I think. She and the kids are staying over at her sister's house." I stop myself. "They should be all right," I tell him; he does not give me an answer as I finish bandaging up my hands and give the box back to him. "So you got any more rooms available?" I ask as he walks to the back room, waving his flashlight. He must not be too comfortable with the dark, I think to myself.

"Yeah, but it hasn't been cleaned yet!" he yells from the room. I chuckle to myself, folding my hands together.

"Does it have four walls and a ceiling that's intact?" I ask him with a smile as he walks back out carrying two bottles of beer. I take one and cringe as I open it and take a long sip for a long day.

"Yes, Sir," he answers.

"Then I could care less if it has been cleaned," I say, taking out my wallet and handing him the money. Before leaving, I tell him I'll only be here one night. He tells me I could stay as long as I like. I thank him, take the room key, and walk to my room. I look through the disfigured window as it sways and breaks apart, creating a small pool inside all those potholes scattered throughout this somewhat empty parking area. I watch the new collection as the tarp folds in on itself and falls swiftly to the bottom cemented ground. I open the door and go into the room and close the door. The smell is potent and dry, causing a low stench to fill the space, the carpeted flooring is stained, and I am almost sure there is a syringe on the sink just before you reach the bathroom. I don't bother to check and dump out the full ashtray into the garbage, which might be the only thing clean in this room tonight. I remove the blankets and sheets and sit them on top of the desk beside the television stand (the screen having a crack is somewhat discerning). I take the pillows off and decide to sleep using the clothes bag as a pillow, not receiving any decent sleep.

I have dreams of that night with Billy and the blood sprayed on the front window. I clear the trickles of blood from my vision, look out the front, and see Sandy lying lifeless in the middle of the road with a cavernous hole in her head. She turns her dead head to face me and smiles. I awaken to the sounds of waves crashing against the shoreline.

I am brought back to Yesteryear and her horrid lies. I check the time, and there should be enough time to take a quick shower and walk to the school. I take out the notebook, leave the bag, and tell Thomas I will return for the sack after school; he answers with a respectful nod. The walk was long and relatively peaceful. I stop by the front office and tell them I am doing fine. They do not try to make polite conversation which seems quite odd to me at first; I ignore this and walk to the classroom, reading through the notebook skimming through old stories, and reading them. "He walks forth, taking the woman's hands, and says to her in all seriousness and courage. *I wish to feel this pain so you know you will never be alone again.* What a joke," I say to myself and read a page with only one sentence that must have been written in my youth. *"In this stunning realization, I have come forth to the stand and stated that I wish to be free to make my conventions and decree that I am responsible for my freedom."* I chuckle to myself as the bell rings and the students enter. There were only twelve; I called roll and noticed that Nancy had not answered me. "Has anyone seen Nancy today?" I ask the classroom. They all say they have not. I mark her absinthe, figuring she must have had a family matter or something to worry about today. I put the logbook down and walked around the desk, standing before the class. "How was everyone's night?" I ask, and they give me groans and complaints about trees being down in their driveways and how much they hate the rain because it makes them tired. After they were done with their stories and tales of woe. I smiled and sat on the lip of my desk. "Well, I'm sorry for anyone actively affected by the storm. Now can anyone tell me why you had that reaction to the question? There is a term I want to know if any of you know it," I say in curiosity, and someone raises their hand. I nod, acknowledging them.

"Negative Bias?" they ask questioningly.

"Good! write that down, and I will speak about the next few things." I give them enough time to get out their notebooks. "Negative Bias is the term psychologists use when our brains carry a strong negative reaction towards something that has no real significance. This reaction also carries on to how you react around your family and friends" they all write this down, and I continue. "One has to wonder, where does negativity come from? I'm here to tell you that the area of the brain called the Prefrontal Cortex stimulates the feeling of anger." They all scribbled in their notebooks as I continued with the lesson for the day, which was based on what angers a human being, or at least what truly makes us angry. It was not just a study of their minds but of their character as well. I have concluded that they are terrified of graduation, boyfriends, and girlfriends ultimately being separated friendships ending. Most would never dream of going off to college. They simply have too many ties with this place that is forever forgotten to time as well with the ground that surrounds the mountains in the east where small towns will soon turn into superpixels be-riding of a world that's long forgotten. Quite the poetic ending, if I do say so myself. The rest of the classes weren't half bad. I discovered that in all the clutter of young imbeciles, there was some light of some level of intelligence in those eyes as I spoke in front of them. I felt a fleeting feeling that I will most likely never feel again, not at least until I retire from this school. I felt freedom. I felt happy once in Yesteryear.

"How was it today, Sam?" Victor asks as I walk into the office as if right in the queue. I smile and shake his hand, and clock out for the day.

"Not half bad actually, not half bad at all," I say. We talk more than usual and find out Victor is a decent fellow. I have been invited to meet his family next week. I walk out of the building. I find it a comfort to call my second home and walk to the nearest waffle joint, which is Harveys, old Harvy makes the best waffles this side of the state. Anyone in town wouldn't tell me differently. I walk in, the bell above the door rings, and Harvey walks out to take my order with a skip in his step. He only greets me this way because I have always tipped him big. I ignore this fact and walk up to sit in front of the line of cooks.

"What are you having, Mr. Dark?" he says in his thick Italian accent.

"I was thinking the house special today, Harv," I smile. Harvey laughs.

"Always you with the special Mr.Dark. Why not get something else besides a steak and eggs with black coffee? I tire off making this," he says, throwing his arms every which way humanly possible.

"Maybe I like the food," I say with a smile. Harvy rolls his eyes and turns to call out the order. I turn to skim over the restaurant and see some new faces. I am glad to see his business ventures working out for him. I turn to the television and ask him to turn it to the News. He does so without question, and I listen in as Chet Downs (I met him once about a year ago at a bar trying to hook up with a sixteen-year-old who somehow made her way into the bar) and Kelly Vermont (she is a decent woman not very bright, however) make their afternoon announcements. Chet is wearing a presentable button-down, his light brown hair slicked back into a man bun, and his infamous gapped front teeth. Kelly is wearing a bright red dress revealing a good amount of cleavage, which causes the men in the restaurant to wolf whistle, even Harvy, who gets smacked in the back of his thinning head by his wife. Who turns out to be a server. I smile and chuckle at this. "You might be in trouble over there, Harv!" I say over the sounds of long potato strips being dropped into a pool of burning oil. Harvey throws up his hands as if unbeknownst to his wrongdoing.

"Can you blame me, eh?" he says through his belly of laughter.

"I am not the man to ask Harvy," I say, pointing to the ring on my finger, and he walks over, making his voice sound as if it were just above a whisper.

"Yeah, but say if you weren't married and that beautiful white woman on that screen came through those doors and asked you out for dinner even if she doesn't know you, even if you are just some bump nobody from the middle of nowhere, would you accept the offer?" He says with a wicked smile spread across his face. I chuckle and lean back into the metal chair, a smile spread across my face.

"Well, if she were to ask me reasonably, then I wouldn't have a choice but to accept the offer because I'm polite like that." This caused Harvy to let out an enormous cackle causing the whole restaurant to jump from their seats and look at him questioningly.

"Oh, that was good, Mr.Dark!" He says through the laughter, wiping away a tear from his cheek. "Polite manner," he says to himself, walking away. I finally turn to the television. Kelly is just now getting to the latest.

"Agony makes its way down Montana Road today as we have just received that Nancy Stephens. A high school student greatly praised by this little community has committed suicide. Leaving behind what is led to believe a letter for the people we have been permitted to read from this letter by the victims' parents. *Suddenly. A child enters the room, sees the three candles no longer burning, and begins to cry, why are you not burning? You are supposed to stay lit until the end! The candle, now old with age, gently speaks to this child, don't be afraid, for I am Hope, and while I still burn. We can relight the other candles of Peace, Faith, and Love, for there is still much to have in this world.* We can all agree that there is still much more hope to have. Our thoughts and prayers go out to this family," I don't bother to start eating my meal, so I get out of my chair and pay for it anyways and walk out of the door, which rings its bells and walk home until later that evening.

I decided to take a short walk down the road where Hope lived and see that from her doorstep to the street corner, bouquets and little gifts for the family when they return. I make my way through the crowd kneeling and saying their silent prayers, stopping at the foot of an old picture of the student and picking it up, and placing a scrap piece of paper on the crest between the glass and the frame. The part of the paper says *Goodbye, Hope.* I sigh and neatly place the picture back down onto the sidewalk and again make my way through the crowd and on my way home. I close the door to a world of black and white and sit in the living room, basking in the dark, huddling myself into a little ball because of the cold breeze through the open cavity in our roof. I am in denial that one of my students committed suicide because of me. Why did I push her so far? Why did I tell her all those terrible things? Maybe I could have fixed this. But, no, I only would have made things worse. How do you know this selfish prick?! You did this. You're the one that killed her! You're the one that pushed her over the edge of the abyss, you damned fool! I lean forward.

"You did this," I say to myself, looking into my reflection. "You killed all three of the only people who seemed to understand," I tell myself in the review. I turn to the seats beside me and see Sandy and Billy sitting there, calm as a butterfly resting on a rose during summer. I look back to the television and see Nancy standing there with a long slash cut horizontally across her neck, causing her pink sweater to lose its color. I bend my head low and whisper. "I'm sorry, I have become so obsessed with finding my reason to live that it has caused yours. I was never a good friend to you, Billy, I was always jealous of your success, and Sandy, I have always respected you. Still, you never showed me any of that, and now I see why. Nancy, I am sorry for bringing you into my world. I'm sorry for what I said that day," I say, looking back up and seeing they have gone. I close my eyes until I am awakened by knocking at the door and go to answer. "Hey," Brittany says, holding a flashlight. "I heard the news and thought you needed some company" I quickly grab her and hug her tightly. "That would make me happy," I say into her shoulder. We stood there for what seemed to be hours on end until we finally settled into the living room, sitting in her favorite comfort chair. "I'm sorry," I say. She leans in, insinuating that she is listening intently. "I'm sorry for not being… prescient. You want to know what I said to that girl the day before she died" she shakes her head. "She came into my classroom and asked me about my character. Why I see the world the way I do, and why I am such a bitter man while I go through what I would like to see as my version of Yesteryear," she signs and folds one hand over the other. "What did you tell her?" I look at her in awe. "I suggested that maybe this is the way I have always been, maybe I am forever destined with the burden of sadness, then she went on about hope, and I told her that there is no more hope for me left to search for anymore. There is only me and my search for justification. That is what killed her, my fucking arrogance and my lack of concern for other emotions" I laugh in bewilderment. "I thought she would be fine. I ignored that she was not in my classroom when I should have gone out and helped her however I could." She leans back and looks at me with a surprising amount of admiration. "I'm glad you told me this. Why have you never spoken of these feelings?" she asks me. "I didn't want you to leave me. I didn't want you to think I had gone mad. I suppose I have a bad habit of that as well. I think of how I believe others would react instead of dealing with the outcome," I say admittedly. "Can I tell you something?" I nod and listen. "You are many things, Samuel Dark, but a killer is not one of them. Sure, you are troubled and are seeking help; you have a caring heart. You just have an odd way of showing it. You tell me you regret telling that poor girl the things you told her is proof enough that shows you have some amount of humanity left," she says. I listen and hang onto every word. "What if there is a time when I no longer have any?" She looks at me and grabs my hand. "Then we will deal with it together," she says with a smile. "I love you" I awaken from the peaceful dream sitting alone in the living room, looking outside into the bright sunny morning, unsure what to believe is real. The illusion itself felt accurate enough, but don't they all? I write down the dream on an empty sheet of paper inside the notebook, walk back into the world, and take the bus to the motel. The school will be canceled for the next three days because of recent events, and a town eulogy is being held at the courthouse (I learned this from the newspapers). Later this evening, I walked into the hotel's front office and paid what was left of my money.

"My God, Samuel, you look rough young man." He takes me by the shoulder, picks up the money, and puts it back into my pocket. "You save this for whatever you wear to that service later this evening." He says, "Hell, I'll even drive you," carrying that old broken smile. I smile back as we leave the building.

"Just take me to the cheapest store you can find," I tell him as he unlocks his truck and turns on the ignition.

"You got it," he says, and we accelerate into traffic. A faint memory of the wreck comes flashing through my mind as if it were a blur as we drive until we reach the supermarket.

"You got a phone on you?" I ask over the radio, which this way only plays 80s classics. He takes his flip phone out of his pocket and hands it over.

"Who are you going to call?" the old man asks. I look at him in admiration and grit.

"My wife, I need to tell her I'm sorry" he doesn't say another word. It goes to voicemail straight away. I sigh and wait to hear the line click, instigating that the other end has started recording. "Hey Brit, I just wanted to say I'm sorry not only for how I treated you but for leaving you in the dark all this time about my feelings. I guess you could say I thought I could deal with them alone, but I started to realize the pain has gotten ever so much worse, and I suppose this is me asking for another chance. No more leaving you in the dark, no more false smiles. I love you. Be sure to remember that once you hear this," I say, closing the phone as we reach the church filled to the brim with townsfolk and teenagers that hardly knew the girl from neighboring towns. I believe even some folk from the city limits are even here. I leave Thomas to the truck and push and shove my way inside the building, standing against the back right wall next to Jesus on the cross, dying for our stupid choices and mistakes.

CHAPTER SEVEN

The stands are complete, and the air is crisp as the preacher stands in front of the sermon, the family standing in front of the closed casket. Finally, the preacher says let us bend our heads to pray, and the whole town, except for myself, bows their heads and says a short but meaningful prayer. Then, they all turn their attention to the preacher on the stand, who begins his service with ranting and ravings around a specific bible verse which I repeat to myself as he continues about how God will come for us all in the end times.

"The Lord will keep you from all harm. He will watch over your life. Psalm 121:7-8" after this stranger is done with the ravings, he invites anyone else in this sea of madness to come forth and announce themselves and give their respects to the family that would stand before them. Three young women went up and shared their sorry for all the times they would bully the poor girl. I would find out that the next group of people hardly knew the girl and paid their respects purely because no one else would, which caused a deep hole in my stomach to the forum. I walk through the crowd and walk up to the stand with my hands pressed on the hardwood stand.

"Hello," I say to the group of people; the room falls silent; the only thing I can hear is the loud but subtle rattle of the trees coming from the open doors. "I won't give you a verse to hold on to for the remainder of your lives. Honestly, I'm not quite sure why I came up here in the first place" her family gives me an odd look. "I guess the only thing there is to say is that she is in a better place, you will get through it, you all are strong, the typical bullshit you're used to hearing. A few of you are troubled, so I'll leave saying Nancy was a bright girl. She was. She had a bright future that was never promised to her. I am sorry you lost her so early in her life," I say, leaving the stand and walking my way down the aisle with every eye in the room burning away at my skin as I leave the building and walk to the next bus stop on its way into the city. I think Sharlin is supposed to return tomorrow, ignoring the empty bus. Ignoring the possibility that I have begun to fall into my form of madness. Missing that I am alone and will forever be alone in this life. Ignoring the fact that none of this matters in the end. Ignoring Yesteryear and her hurtful truths and her deadly lies.

Once inside the city limits, I get off this bus in front of one of the old broken buildings that used to be a health clinic before they shut it down sometime between now and 2000. I once knew the man who would run this place, his name was Simon, and he is most likely dead now. He and this building have been forgotten like all things that spring from the past. Like myself and the world around me as I stand on this empty sidewalk in a vacant city that has lost all sensation of color. There is only Yesteryear left behind. I continue down the strip until I reach the market store and go inside. This is the only store far the eyes can see that is filled to the roof with green surrounding me; I stroll down the aisle as I collect bread, peanut butter, and a small jelly. I walk to the front of the store, pay for my items, and hike up the strip until I am confident about where I am going, a pawn shop. I go into the store, grab three movies from the half-dollar rack (Goodfellas, The Truman Show, Groundhog Day), and place them on the glass just above some cheap knock-off jewelry. I look at the wall and choose my selection. "I want that one," I say, pointing at the Glock 19.

"Do you have a license to carry?" asks the man who wears the poorly fitted wig.

"It's just for protection," I say demandingly.

"Still, you need a license to carry. If you have that, you can get the gun," the salesman says. "Now you can get a license by appointment with this guy I know, Larry. He works for the PD a few blocks from here, Larry is a decent fellow, and he should give you one without hesitation, but if he sees something up, then no luck. Would you like me to call and ask?" I nod, agreeing, and he calls the officer's number. We stand that way for hours until the officer picks up. "Yeah, hey Larry, It's Joe. I've got this guy looking for a license to carry. What's your name?" He says, leaning over the glass. I answer. "He says his name is Samuel James Dark. What is your reason for wanting to carry a firearm?" I think about this for a moment.

"Protection, there have been a lot of things happening to our neighbors in the area I live in. I just don't want that happening without having something to protect my wife and kids." Joe takes the phone off of the speaker.

"Did you get all of that? Good," he says, taking the phone into the other room. "Yeah, the fax machine still works," he says with a snarky tone as I stand in the middle of the room. He comes back into the room with a sheet of paper in hand. "He says there is a lot more to do with this type of thing, but since Larry checked your record and sees that it is perfect, not even a driving ticket. He has decided to just let you have a printed copy instead of going through the trouble of coming in and going through the whole process of getting one of these." He says, handing me the piece of paper. I fold it and put it into my back pocket as he goes to the wall and collects my chosen gun. "Okay, you can have this in your car in your home, but don't, and I mean you don't carry it where the cops can make out its features. I would suggest putting it behind your shirt until you get home." He bends over to get what seems to be a pretty heavy box of rounds, takes out the clip, loads them one by one, puts the magazine back in, and flips on the safety. "Fully loaded. Be sure to be responsible," he says, handing me the weapon. I untuck the front of my shirt, put the gun to the side of my stomach, put the loose flap of cloth over the gun, pay for my items using a card, not cash, and walk out of the store.

I take the bus back to the hotel and stop by the front office. I apologize to Thomas for how I acted earlier in the day; he scoffs, waves me off, and walks to the back room, pouring himself a cup of coffee. He had always preferred his with an overbearing amount of creamer and offered me a cup. I ask him to make mine black, and he does, stating his disdain for the aftertaste that all black coffee leaves in the throat. We laugh and crack jokes with one another for a little while, and I ask him to borrow the truck tonight. He gives me the keys and tells me to drive safely. I turn to him.

"I plan to," and exit the office leaving behind a half glass of all-black coffee, retreat into the room, and take a nap setting the timer to wake me up later this evening. When the alarm goes off, I rip off a long cloth from the bed sheet and wrap it around my head, covering my mouth. This is ridiculous, I tell myself. You don't need the money. I look in the mirror and pull down the loosely tied mask. What would they think of this? I ask myself.

"You're a fool," I tell myself in the mirror. I grab the gun and look at the once-empty chair seeing Nancy sitting there with a displeased look in her eyes. "I'm sorry," I say to her as I grab the keys, exit the room, unlock the truck, and sit in a daze. I look over at the passenger seat and see myself looking back into my eyes pleadingly. The cloth mask was removed, and the bags underneath my eyes were no longer there. I look healthy. "We don't have to do this. We don't have to go down this road," the aberration says, looking on in discontent. I put my head on the steering wheel. "I know, but maybe I will feel something, anything. Maybe I will find my justification?" I suggest looking back up to the aberration, which has disappeared. I put the truck in reverse, back up into the parking lot, and put it into drive. I go to the nearest gas station, park a block from the store, and scope the area using the rearview mirror. "You don't have to do this."

I remind myself to take out the gun, take the safety off, and get out of the truck. I will lock it and walk into the store quickly, pulling out the gun and aiming it at the young woman running the register.

"Money!" I scream as I pull back the hammer. "I'm sorry," I say in a timid, fearful manner as she does what I say and opens the register taking out some ten-dollar bills and some change and handing them over the counter. I grab the money and tuck it into my pockets. The Employees Only door opens and comes out. The store owner is carrying what looks to be a pump action shotgun. He loads it and fires it at my head as I leap behind the chip aisle causing him to miss. Again, I jump in fear as the chips fill the store with little explosions. "Fuck!" I scream through the mask as I try to crawl slowly to the back door. This man in the red and black checkered shirt strolls to my aisle, loading his gun as he does so.

"Friend, I don't know who you are, but I know you had two choices!" he announces as I crawl into the snack aisle he had just passed. I look up at the young woman and motion for her to keep quiet. She nods, almost terrified, as she screams as he shoots the grounds from which I come. "You chose wrong," he says, running around the aisle and turning to me, aiming down his shotgun. I close my eyes and quickly aim and shoot the man in the left shoulder, causing the woman to whale and exit the building in fear. I hurriedly got onto my feet and walking over to this man.

"I'm sorry," I say, taking the money out of my pocket and laying it beside his gun. "This should cover your visit to the hospital," I say coldly as I walk out of the store, rush to the truck, stand on the footstool, and look up the block. "Shit!" I say, cursing as I see blue and red lights flashing.

I quickly get in the truck and take off the mask. Then, putting the car into gear, I retreat from the scene heading back to the hotel. I look back to the passenger side and see Billy sitting there, almost in a daze, looking as if he is lost.

"Are you going to tell me I didn't have to do that either, or are you going to tell me something like, oh Sam, this isn't the way to do things?!" I yell in a fit of anger. I look back to the road and see the hotel is just a few minutes out. "Billy, you've got to give me something, anything that could tell me why I'm here" Billy's cold decrepit face turns, looks at me with his frozen dead eyes, and shakes his head. I received the message clearly and continued to drive. I stop by the front desk before going to my room. Thomas tells me there are a few messages for me on the phone when I get to the room. Still, I don't bother to ask where he got this information concluding that he has monitored the rooms. I dismiss this with the thought of it being an invasion of privacy. I thank him and walk to my room, leaving the keys on the counter. I put the gun safely in one of the drawers underneath the television and played the messages.

"Hey Samuel, this is Sharlin. I was just calling to tell you that I am back in town and would like you to come to buy the old stomping ground tomorrow morning, perhaps? I have a feeling we have a lot to discuss regarding recent events. I just think it would be good for you to talk about it, and if you are comfortable, I would also like your wife to be there with you. I have realized that you have been going through some sort of conflict. I just want to see if there is a way to fix this. Anyways I better get going; I hope to see you tomorrow! Have a good rest of your day!" she says, ending the call, and the following message plays.

"Hey. Sam. I got a call from that therapist; honestly, I don't know how to feel about that. Would you want me there?" I pick up the phone and redial the number, which goes to voicemail.

"I don't have to explain myself, but yeah, sure. I would like that. A lot, actually" I put the phone down and lie down for a sleepless night. At some point in the night, I get up and take my notebook with me as I sit outside on the curb and watch the sunrise. The rising sun leaves a melodic serenity of orange, pink, and blue serenity, conversing with one another into a sea of eternal bliss. Then it was gone. That moment of peace has vanished as quickly as it came, and now I am forever stuck here in this sea of Yesteryear. I get off the curb and go back into the office. "Hey, Thomas," he stops me dead in my tracks, and my body falls stiff with fear.

"You don't have to say it. I heard everything on the phone. Take it and go," Thomas says, waving me off. I take the keys off the counter and crank up the truck, setting the notebook in the passenger seat. I close my eyes and take several controlling breaths to help calm my nerves. I put the car in drive and travel through town, sure to take in the buildings and the people that reside in them because they, too, will eventually be taken by the wrath of their searches for justification through this never-ending journey through Yesteryear. Once inside, I noticed that the painting I had mistakenly taken for being an original had been replaced by a portrait of a black line surrounded by colorful blotches of paint scattered about. I go over to the sign-in sheet and kneel close to the window, ensuring that the nurse on the other end can hear the inflection in my voice. "Where is the other painting?" I ask, realizing this is not the moderately attractive nurse who spoke with me before. This one seems to be much older and wiser with her words.

"It was removed in place of what you see before you," she says, motioning to the new painting on the wall. "It's a shame, really. I liked the painting before; it had so much life to it. But this one just seems" she can no longer come up with a subtle way of saying it, so I decided to take it upon myself and end the sentence for her.

"Sad in a way," I say with a half-crooked smile as I stroll to the waiting area and wait while my left leg begins to jump on its own. I look at the other chairs in the room and see all three of them looking into my soul, my very fiber of being pleading. I can almost hear their voices telling me this is a good decision. Shouldn't I determine this? I wouldn't be here if I didn't think I needed help. But I'm too stubborn even to go against my wishes. Sharlin walks around the corner and throws her arms in the air, and I get out of the chair and walk over to give her a friendly, warm hug. "Sorry, I haven't showered in about a day now," I whisper. She nods and leads me into the room as I carry the notebook folded in half. Even though this room is not the same, the couch has been moved to the other side of the wall, and her desk is now a few feet away from the door's opening. She goes over and takes her seating arrangements. I walk into the room and make my own. We sat there for hours until Brittany walked into the room carrying her purse and wearing an Old Navy sweater; she didn't wake up on time. This thought causes a flash of what I assume to be an estranged look across my face. Brittany looks at me disapprovingly and walks into the room, taking the chair to the right of the couch.

"Hey Brittany," I wave to her, and she answers, giving me a haphazard wave.

"I'm so glad you both have found the time to talk with me today. If you don't mind, Samuel, I would like to brief your wife on your current situation," she suggested.

"She already knows about my condition," I say.

"All right, I want to talk about your home life these past few days. Have you noticed any behavior change, Brittany?" she asks, looking over to my wife, who hesitates before answering.

"Yes, over time we lived together, he was slowly becoming cold and bitter. But he wasn't home when he walked through those doors. Sam might have been able to hide it from the kids, but he could never hide it from me. That was why we left, he never talked about the problem, and when he did, he would always change the subject," she says. Sharlin quickly writes down her notes.

"Why did you never push the subject?" Sharlin asks.

"Because I was afraid. Not of Sam. I was afraid of what he would do to himself," she says worryingly. I take this in, rubbing my hands together, the scar tissue sporadic, as if dancing to give the queen of the ball a *"REAL"* show on the dancefloor.

"I did do something not just to myself but others," I say, and they both look at me with worried curiosity.

"After you left, just before the storm, I cut myself. Not out of sadness or anger but because I felt I deserved that pain. After that, the storm blew a tree over, causing a new hole to form in the roof. I'm honestly not entirely sure if the house still stands. Now I am staying in a Hotel, and the owner was nice enough to let me stay as long as I would like. I got these while trying to fight my way through that storm," I say, holding up my hands for them to see. "All that trouble, just for a place to sleep," I say, chuckling.

Sharlin scoots her chair closer to us and leans forward. "Samuel, have you been taking your medication?" I shake my head no. "Why?" she asks.

"They would just make the pain worse. But, I will be the first to admit that after I threw them out, I have been prone to some erratic behavior," I say coldly.

Brittany scoffs. "What sort of erratic behavior?" she asks.

I lean close to the group. "That gas station that was robbed the other night was me. I didn't want to hurt that man, but what explanation does one go for when explaining the criminal defending himself to the authorities? Sure, that would look fine on paper, but people would suggest different things. I didn't want to rob that store. It just happened. I suppose I just wanted to feel something, anything really," I say admittedly.

"Sharlin, in doctoral terms, would you call this an act of erratic behavior?" Brittany turns, giving me a disgusted look, whereas Sharlin looks at me as if studying me.

"Any act of violence against oneself or another is always considered irrational, Samuel," she answers. "May I see that notebook of yours? I think your wife would like to hear your story," she says, and I hand over the notebook. "How far have you read in the story Brittany?" she asks, looking over to my wife.

"The title," Brittany answers. They take the notebook and walk outside the door, reading it with one another. I close my eyes, daydreaming of sandy beaches and the water washing its way between my toes as I sit there watching the rise and fall of the tides. I am taken out of my dream once I hear the door shut, and they both walk in, Brittany gives me the notebook, and I sit it in my lap and hide it from the rest of the world. They both take their seats. Sharlin writes down a few notes and looks at me in admiration.

"What does the title Yesteryear mean to you, Samuel?" Sharlin asks; I look behind her. All three of them standing before me, Billy, Sandy, and Nancy, all victims of Yesteryear and her hurtful ways, I genuinely feel their deaths are my faults alone. All standing straight, one buy one. "Samuel?" Sharlin says questioningly. "What do you see?" I look at her in fear and quickly look over to Brittany, who gives me the same worrying gaze the whole room gives me. I sit there hyperventilating, trying to take a more controlled breath as a voice comes through in a haze as visions of my past bring themselves forthwith. Flashes go by obtaining images of the dead bodies. I caused the crash, I killed Sandy, and I mutilated Nancy's body. This is my admission of guilt. I close my eyes and wait for Yesteryear to call my name.

CHAPTER EIGHT

The room falls silent until that silence is overtaken by a truck going down the highway. I open my eyes to find myself in front of the mail carrier; I roll down the window slowly to the base of the door. I feel the gust of wind against my face as I look into the world around me. It was all a dream. I ask myself as I put my head back in the truck and look forward; the wind stops. I look back to the window to find it closed. I try to roll it back down, but the handle is stuck in time. This is the dream, I tell myself as I look at the driver.

"Billy?" I ask questioningly, looking at the clear-faced man, reminded of the blood and the sound of the horn going off infinitely.

"Nope, I'm the queen of England," he says, laughing alone at his joke; I raise my eyebrows in surprise as I look forward to seeing that we are slowly going into the left lane.

"None of this is real, is it?" I ask the vision, and he answers with a slow shake of the head.

"Pretty much, old buddy." He says with an oppressive enthusiasm. "None of it is real, never has been, and never will be. There is only here, wherever you put us," he says.

"How many times must I see this day? How many days of Yesteryear will I have to relive?" So I say as I see two lights coming down this empty highway.

"I don't know. Hopefully, you will figure something out soon. Otherwise, we're both going to be here for a while." Billy says as my body jumps for the wheel, causing the back of the red truck to crash against the semi-truck, causing the red truck to flip and skid onto its side. I close my eyes. "Well, that hurt," Billy says beside me. I open my eyes, and we are back inside the truck speeding down the highway. I look him up and down, seeing he isn't harmed.

"None of it is real," I tell myself, forcing myself to be at ease. "Why here?" I ask him, and he shrugs his shoulders.

"I wouldn't know. It's your fantasy, old boy, you tell me." I take this in for a moment.

"I don't know," I say as the truck crashes into the semi-truck again.

"We have to stop meeting like this," he says with his old whimsical arrogant tone. I chuckle at this, realizing the longevity of the situation.

"So this is it?" I ask.

"Yep, nothing more to it than this, nothing too much that's better," he says honestly, looking in front of us and seeing the truck.

"I'm sorry for what happened that day," I say, looking at him from the corner of my eye.

"It wasn't your fault. We were both young and stupid. I was the only one responsible for my death, not you. But, hell, you tried saving both of us. That's something to be proud of," he says with admiration. "I'm proud of you, Sam, I am. You have done the impossible. You are coming back to reality," he says as we drive closer to the truck that will inevitably cause his death. I ready myself to grab the wheel. Billy places his large hand across my chest. "You can't save someone already dead. This moment in Yesteryear, it's fixed. It can never be changed, no matter how much you want it to. Your search for justification, well, I'm sorry to tell you there is nothing to look for. Once you realize that, maybe you can find some peace," he says, looking on as the glass grows bright.

"Justification. I wonder if there is such a thing," Billy says, closing his eyes as the white light overtakes the truck. I open my eyes, looking back at the symmetry in front of Billy's tombstone. I sit up to the sounds of levees breaking, followed by the scattering of small rocks. As I listen to the heavy footfall approaching me, I see Sandy descending the hill.

"Well, don't you look like shit," she says, breathing heavily. Then, finally, she stops kneeling, takes a few hasty breaths, and brings herself forward. I get off the ground and dust myself off.

"I wasn't up here when you died," I say, looking at the stone that no longer carries a name or a date of death. I look at this questioningly.

"You don't remember," she says as the gun appears in my hand. "The mind. It can be dangerous, especially when you're not sure what's real," she says, turning to the tomb. "I suppose you want me to tell you it wasn't your fault, but your mind won't let me. I guess you already got that lesson," she says, taking the old revolver out of my hand and getting the bullets ready.

."What am I supposed to learn from all of this?" I ask her.

"I won't know till you tell me, Sam. I thought you would have already taken that much from all this mess" she closed the chamber and spun the bullet wheel. "We both can stay here till you decide on something for me to teach you besides all the parts of the brain. I've got all the time in the world in here" she says, bringing the gun to the side of her head and pulling the trigger. Blood smears the side of the tomb; I close my eyes quickly and wait for Sandy to make her journey up the hill.

"Did you learn something?" she asks. I shake solemnly. "What did Billy say before you came here?" She decides to ask.

"My search for justification means nothing, Yesteryear. My untold story means nothing," I say, sitting back on the grass, crushing the leaves. Sandy does the same.

"There is no story being told here, Sammy. That's the point, we crawl to the depths of hell and climb the tallest of mountains, searching for something determined that whatever we are searching for is our true meaning. There is none. There is no good or bad ending to a life, it depends on what you do while you're alive that matters," she says. I think back to the gas station and the bullet I put into that man's shoulder, causing the truck to crash murder.

"I've done some bad things, Sandy," I say, admittedly.

"I know. We all have. You just have to live with it," Sandy says, pointing the gun to the side of her head, and she pulls the trigger. I close my eyes again, and we are back in the same position. "I guess you learned something after all." She says, pointing the gun at my head. "This might hurt a little," she says slightly hesitantly. "Are you ready?" she asked me.

"Yes. I am no longer afraid" I close my eyes.

"Good," Sandy says; my ears go deaf at the gunshot sound. I open my eyes, still defined by the sound of eternal nothingness. I hear something through the smog of sounds and wavelengths; the room is painted white with little areas of pink. I look around and see a pink dresser. All the standard appliances of a young teenage girl's bedroom are colored pink except for the walls and the carpeting. I get off the mattress and fix the bed sheets. I walk over to the pink desk to find a red journal; I pick up this book and open it to see the empty pages. I sit the journal back on the desk and look out the window to a more colorful world than the one I left behind. Vibrant, rich colors jump out at me as I try opening the window only to find that it too has been trapped to time, the house is silent, and no one seems home. Why here? I wonder to myself as I sit back down on the bed. I look at the clock seeing that it has been turned off. The door opens slowly.

"I'm glad you could make it," Nancy says warmly.

"Of course," I say. "Nancy, I fear I have truly gone mad with this search for a justification, and I fear that I will never stop looking for it.

I'm afraid. I'm afraid of what else I will do to others, and what I will lead them to. All I ever wanted was to find something, feel something that would tell me what my purpose is here," I say to this figment of my discontented imagination. "I haven't found a way to end my tail of Yesteryear," I say admittedly.

"Is that truly what you are looking for? A way to end your story untold?" she asks me, almost in spite and anger.

"Yes, I don't know. I don't want to end the story," I say admittedly.

"Why not?" she asks me as she pulls a knife from thin air and rests the blade's tip at the base of her throat. "It is a good tale of a man unconcerned with the world around him," she says hastily.

"But that is not the truth. The untold story is not about a man unconcerned with the world around him. It is a story of an honest telling of a lie mixed with what truth he has to live with, which is bare to none. The truth and the lies have come to a crossroads for this man, who is unhappy with the results. Therefore he becomes withered and bitter to the rest of these false smiles as he searches the lands of Yesteryear for something that is just the truth. It is not a tale of a man who no longer cares for the world. It is one of the men coming to terms with the world and her hurtful lies," I say coldly.

"What is the outcome of this man?" she asks.

"I'm not so sure," I chuckle. "It hasn't been told yet," I say, smiling up at Nancy as she lets the knife go. It falls slowly to the carpeted flooring.

"Then finish it," she says with a smile, engulfing the room with pure bright light. I close my eyes and wait until I open them again. I slowly raise the curtains to find myself back in the room. "Can I finish the story before I tell you?" I ask the both of them, and they both nod, agreeing. I pick up the notebook and ask for a pen. Sharlin gives me a green ballpoint pen. Ignoring this, I jump back into the tale of Yesteryear.

Monday: I became hurtful to Pink for the rest of her days in Yesteryear. I became cold and bitter to the touch of the woman I loved. What a fool I once was in Yesteryear. This would come back to face me, taking the form of fate. I hadn't seen Pink on that day in Yesteryear. Perhaps I could have reasoned with her. Maybe I would have made things worse. However, I came to her eulogy out of respect for the girl. The aisles were filled with false smiles in Yesteryear, and the ones that went onto the stand gave their condolences half-heartedly. I felt sorry for her family, who is now consumed by the gray surrounding the rest of this cruel world of Yesteryear. I gave it all I had, but they called my comments hurtful, so they banished me, sending me back into the world with the rest of those false smiles. Before returning to my stay, I stopped by a martyr and purchased a new pen from his expansive collection. Telling him to have a good day in Yesteryear, I take the pen home and hide it in a safe where no false smiles could reach. I decided to take my mask from hiding, ride up to the cliffside, and look out into this world consumed by Yesteryear as the false smile burns inside that eternal flame. Finally, I feel at peace with the world around me. No more false smiles surround me.

I close the pen and close my eyes. The room falls silent.

I feel nothing.

I click the pen once more.

Way back in Yesteryear.

I close my eyes once more.

I feel nothing. This must be different! She told me I would find something after I finished the story. Yet there is nothing. Not even the satisfaction of a story's ending. There is no resolution to this pain. Nothing, I feel nothing.

"Samuel?" my wife says, looking at me in a fearful, questioning way, "What does it mean?" Sharlin asks, leaning forward in her chair.

"I don't know. The story continues; I thought I had come to a resolution. I thought Yesteryear would finally end. But it continues. I still search for justification. They lied to me. All three of them carry what is no longer a feasible thing for me. Hope." I get off the couch, take my notebook with me, and they sit back in their chairs. "I have to go," they both try to stop me as I rush through the door and down the stairs in a hurry. I run to the truck, search the glove compartment, and find nothing besides old bills and brochures. I take the keys out of my pocket, rush to the driver's door, and unlock the door; they both come running out, calling my name. I silence their calls with the engine's crank and put it into drive. The truck jumps as I run it over a large grass bed into the main road. I skip the red lights as I drive to the motel. Why? Why has nothing happened? I ask myself as I clear off the bed of sweat that sits above my brows. One droplet falls in my left eye, causing it to sting.

The world goes black, and I am awakened by the sound of the truck horn. The airbag blinds me. I push it out as I get out of the truck, rolling onto the street. Thomas emerges from the building, waving and dancing around like a madman. I can hear all the swearing through the faint ringing in my ears. "I'm sorry," I say under my breath. "I'm so sorry," I say, limping to the room as Thomas pushes me forward, causing me to fall flat onto my stomach. I crawl on as Thomas stomps his foot down onto my spine. I scream in pain and get onto my feet. "I will pay you back!" I cry as I shove him onto his back. Two more vehicles pull up and park horizontally in the lot; one woman each comes out of the car and comes rushing forward. I fall onto the door as I unlock it. I fall onto the shag carpeting and get back onto my two feet. I get the gun out of the drawer, limp back outside, and fire two shots into the plastic roofing that shadows me from the sun.

"Stay back!" I say, pointing the gun at both figures as my hearing slowly returns, folding its way through each cavern. "I'm sorry," I say as I push myself against one of the pillars holding the shade. "I'm sorry," I say to both figures as they slowly walk forward, each surrendering their hands. I slowly slid down the pole, sitting against it with my back pressed against its base. "I just wanted to feel something, anything other than pain. Once that went away, I thought I would be happy, but now I am torn. I have nothing to feel anymore, I have no more reason to search for justification, and yet I still haven't found purpose," I say to the figure closest to me. "Tell me, have I gone mad?" I ask the blonde figure. The figure kneels beside me and takes my hand. "I have nothing more to hold onto anymore," I say. "I have nothing but Yesteryear" I look up at Brittany. "Did you bring the notebook?" She rushes back to her car and brings me the notebook and a pin to finally end the story of a once-happy man.

What is value? Is it what one is worth, or is it simply another lie Yesteryear tells us when we are young and full of color? The question may never be answered with the utmost honesty, but I have told you my tale. I have shared my story, yet I feel indifferent about the ending. There still seems to be none in sight. I grab my new pen.

CLICK… went to the old world… CLICK went Yesteryear and her lies of a better world. After all, this is done. After a story's end, perhaps I will find value elsewhere. Maybe I will finally wear that smile once again. Onto you, I give my account to do with as you wish. I have no reason to worry anymore. I am free to roam the stars like the ones before me. I wonder what life is like after Yesteryear. Maybe there is nothing. My heart is open to infinite possibilities as my spirit leaves, descending into that shallow light. Finally, I will be happy once more.

Way back in Yesteryear.

Sharlin is the first to read the completed story. After she is done, she hands the notebook to Brittany.

"What does Yesteryear mean to you, Samuel?" They both ask instinctively. I look at them both in disapproval and chuckle. Then, I look over at Thomas, who slowly stands onto his feet and rushes over, ranting and raving like a mad dog. Sharlin takes the man and walks him over to his car, telling him she could cover the cost of repairs to his truck. Brittany walks over and sets the notebook between us, sighing with relief.

"I thought I lost you there," she says timidly.

"You didn't lose me. I lost myself," I say admittedly. Brittany leans over and gives me a bear hug.

"I've missed you," she says, whispering. Tearfully I trust away from the hug.

"I'll miss you too," I say to her.

The world falls silent.

CLICK… went Yesteryear.

She is lying in a pool of her blood now. I'm sorry, Brittany. So very sorry. The police pick me up and drag me to the police cruiser, slamming my head against its cold hood. I stare at the body of my former wife just lying there, Sharlin standing beside her, crying in pain. The world was silent when they put me in the car. I didn't pay attention during my trial. The judge took pity on me though I was not so sure I deserved it. The judge decided to give me a month back in the psychiatric facility. My doctor would be Sharlin, and a fellow named Michael, who was good at his job. He was so good they had to mention his master's in psychiatry twice. That means he is twice as good at his job.

I agreed with the judge. After my trial period, they would have the journey determine my fate. Funny, I have never been one to enjoy knowing my outcome. They led me to a van and had me sit in the back, people outside the truck proclaiming their hatred for me. I close my eyes and dream of the sands until we reach the facility. I am awakened by the two guards driving this van via them opening the door. I am greeted by Sharlin and a tall lengthy man with slick brown hair who holds out his hand for me to shake. I lift my chained-bound hands. He turns his head away.

"Jesus Christ, people, can we not show some common human decency for our new guest?" He walks over and lowers his voice. "I am sorry about this," he says, motioning for the guard to hand over the keys. The guard does so without question. The man, whom I assume to be Doctor Michael, smiles as he unlocks the chains. I move my legs around, getting used to my newfound freedom. I could get used to this, I think to myself as I look up at this man's smile. He turns in a showman-like fashion. "Please let me show you around your new home for the next month." I quickly look down at this stranger's name tag. My assumption is correct. This man is Michael, who carries a wide grin as we walk to my new fortitude. I lean over to Sharlin.

"Is this it?" I ask her.

"Yes," she says coldly, taking a few quick, concise steps ahead of the good doctor and me. I look at this tall light brown building, the windows bordered with long strips of iron connected to cement. This is where I will stay for the next few months. So I might as well get used to the building itself. The inside of the building is a cool white, and it looks like no one has been in these halls for quite some time. My body grows cold and shivers as I compare it to the school. The doctor claps me on the shoulder.

"Don't worry, I will answer all your questions in time, but for now, my friend, you must rest. Your room is this way," he says, leading down a long corridor passing other rooms, which I don't pay any attention to. "Samuel James Dark, a former high school psychology teacher, graduated with high honors, a former diagnosis done by doctor Sharlin Gwentonskey. The diagnosis given was chronic depression. The new diagnosis shows that mister Dark suffers from schizophrenia, and judging by your record, you have always had this. More recently, you have claimed it has gotten worse over time. This could result in the actions you have taken leading you here. Does that sound right to you?" he talked to himself more than anyone in the hall.

"Why are you trying to help me?" I ask this man as we come to our assumed stopping point.

"Because Samuel, not only is it my job, but you interest me," he says with a smile. "Now get some rest. We will talk more in the morning," he says. I was ushered into the room and sat on the side of the bed. "Here, a gift," he says, handing me a new notebook. "Don't worry, I won't ask you to show me any of your writing." He says as one of the guards brings in a tall stand with a camera mounted on top of it; he sits it down quickly and plugs it in. "I forgot to mention that you will be recorded by this camera you see before you and the one in that top right-hand corner." I look up as he sets up a camcorder on the table's far side; two cameras are on both top-end corners of the room. "I wouldn't mind those. We use them to monitor you during your, how you would say. Episodes" I nod my head slowly and sit the notebook beside me. "Don't worry. You will be able to make this room your own. I will have someone come in here with some paint to give you something to do," he smiles as the door closes. I stare as they walk past the window of the door. Then, I look back up to the camera seeing Brittany with a hole piercing her stomach.

"Please leave me alone," I say, closing my eyes as the lights dim.

YESTERYEAR: Lucy

We seek out the things we think we need most in this life. The sooner we get there we realize how foolish this pursuit has become. Yet we find a way to hang on to Lucy and her lies. One has to wonder; somebody has to ask. Why?

CHAPTER NINE

The room is silent, and the white walls are cold. That might be the room itself, I think to myself as I look up to the top left corner of the room, watching as that light continuously blinks red. One…two…three, I think to myself, counting the blinking of this almost hypnotizing light. Knock, knock, knock. Michael walks into the room without me giving him an answer. He comes in briskly, sitting in his chair across the table, sitting down a suitcase and some mechanical device with some dials turned. He unlocks the briefcase, taking out my file, his reading glasses, and a clipboard with some scratch paper on it.

"How are we feeling today, mister Dark?" Michael asks.

"Samuel. My name is Samuel," I say, coldly shivering while playing with my thumbs.

"Ahh, first name basis, we're already making headway," he chuckles. "All right, Samuel, this little toy of ours monitors your brainwaves; it's not a lie detector you see in all those movies nowadays. It's more so used to detect any anomalies in your thought process. For example, let's say you start seeing things that are not there or feeling things with no mass. This little gadget here will detect that anomaly. Don't worry, it's completely harmless" he takes out a little bag with suction cups in it with the paper still on them and passes them over the table. "I would ask that you place two on each corner of the front of your head and two more on each of your cheeks." He says, pointing to all these areas. I open the small bag and take out four ripping the paper off them one by one and sticking them in place. Michael nods approvingly. "Now it's my turn to lead us in this little waltz of ours." He says, getting up from his chair and kneeling, hooking the tiny receivers to the suction cups and turning two dials. The needle rises and falls. "All right," Michael says, sitting across from me. "Is your name Samuel James Dark?" Michael asks professionally, and I might as well show this same respect toward the man.

"Yes," I say with a cold gaze.

"Are you aware of where you are and the testing we are doing today?" he says similarly.

"Yes, I know where I am, and I think we are both here for one simple reason. To prove that I should be let back out into the world. Despite what I have done." Like the quick flash of a polaroid camera, memories of Yesteryear bring themselves forward. Crashing the truck, shooting Sandy, slashing Nancy's throat, shooting my wife. "Can I ask you a question?" Michael looks at me as if he has already planned for this question. "What will happen to my children?" the needle rises as I hear the sounds of crashing waves and a woman singing a song I have never heard before. Michael sighs, taking notes on the anomaly shown on this device.

"Well, not to open any past scars, but to consider that their mother is now deceased and their father is. For lack of a better word, indisposed. So your kids will be sent to foster care. So don't worry; they will find an apt family for the duo and be together throughout the process. Now back to the question. How long have you been aware of your medical condition?" he asks curiously.

"Since I was a child. Pretty early on, I would often find an escape from any trouble I was having," I answer honestly.

"Do you know anyone in your family history with a similar mental illness?" he asks. I try to think of the last time we had a family reunion, I was ten at the time, and nobody seemed to be off. However, they all wore their careless false smiles. Mask, always the mask they tie on in their mornings.

"No, not that I can think of," I answer.

"All right, Samuel, two more questions, then you can return to your room. With your first evaluator, you were tasked with completing your own story, which you titled Yesteryear. When asked about the story and its meaning, you often give a vague answer, so tell me. Is Yesteryear another story in an old notebook, or does it hold something deeper? Maybe you saw it as something that would give you purpose. Is that it, Samuel? Are you just a sick man seeking a cure?" the room falls silent. "Samuel, I can't start helping you until you give me some answers," he says, leaning over the table and keeping his voice low and calm.

"There is only one thing I am seeking now," he looks into my eyes curiously. "I seek to forgive myself for what I have done. I can no longer live with the pain I caused others for much longer. I no longer seek my purpose. I didn't feel anything upon the story completion in Yesteryear when I wished I did. I have never believed in fate, though I suppose this is just that. The fate of one Samuel James Dark. Knowing I will die, I'm unsure how to feel about that." The needle stops jumping, and the rabbit has finally lost energy and fallen asleep.

"This was a good session today Samuel, and I look forward to talking with you more. There will be dinner waiting for you in your room, along with a ball. Unfortunately, we can't give you any contact with anyone beyond that wall. Hence, I apologize for the lack of phone service." I smile lightly, taking in the newfound warmth of the room as he presses the red button beside the door, which connects to the ceiling. "Guard, please send someone to room A15 to retrieve our guest and take him back to his room," letting go of the button, he turns his attention back to me. "Oh, by the way, once you're done with your food, just wave down the camera!"

I nod as the door unlocks and opens from the outside. This guard sporting a mustache and a broad chest, steroids, I think to myself in a light chuckle as I take off the suction cups and unhook them from the wires. I throw the suction cups away as I leave the room. The guard and I walk the hall in silence.

"So, how long have you been working here?" I ask. Nothing; this man's stoneface keeps on; the only way to break this barrier is a good joke. "Say, Chuck, why did the frog take the bus to work today?" Silence yet again. "His car got toad away," I chuckle, yet he does not. "All right, I see. I'm not a big fan of that one. Fine then, how do poets say hello? Hey, haven't we metaphor? Still nothing?" I say as we reach closer to my room at the end of the hallway. "Last one," he does not answer. "What kind of tea is hard to swallow?" I ask this man as I stop dead in the center of the road.

Cars crash into one another, and a child is a few feet away. I quickly dash away from this guard after the child who jumps off the side of the freeway. "No!" I scream as a car flings me onto my back. I turn my head, seeing my legs crushed under a red truck's front bumper; it has a sticker WYOMING STATE; it reads, I fall out of this dream seeing the cool light of the sky as the guard pins me to the ground. "I have to save him," I say; my breath comes out a hiss. I hear a door open behind us.

"What is the meaning of this?!" Michael says, pushing the guard off me. I continue to lie down as Michael bickers at this guard for manhandling me; the guard explains that I was close to jumping, and the world falls silent as I get onto my feet. "Samuel, what did you see?" Michael asks, putting his hand on my shoulder.

"I didn't mean to do it," I say, watching the clouds slowly pass over the building. "How are you certain that this will help me?" I ask, looking back at Michael, whose cold demeanor surprises me. "How will you help me?" I ask.

"Any way I can. It's not just me here. Sharlin though her morals say otherwise, she is here to help you too," he says almost assuredly. "We will give you a few minutes alone up here. Then, once you're ready, I'd like for you to come back down with me," he says, lightly pushing the guard and ushering the guard back down the stairs.

"How do you know I won't jump!" I ask as he crosses the doorway.

"I trust you will make the right decision eventually," he says in an almost meaningful way that nearly makes me believe him for a split second. He was correct. I decided to go back down the stairs and into my room to enjoy a lovely meatloaf. Bonk...catch with the left hand...Bonk... see with the right, this ball feels nice and has written on its side. This writing I cannot understand though I do not care.

I roll the ball in my hands until I fall fast to sleep. There isn't a knock this time to awaken me. I stand up and dust myself off, push the locked door, slam my left shoulder into it, and hold my shoulder for a long moment.

"Hey!" I yell, waving my arm toward the camera. "Is there something wrong with the door?" I say, slamming my other shoulder into the door, causing it to crash open and leading to me falling onto the floor and blacking out. When I awaken, I stand quickly and look down the corridor. "Oh, my God!" I say, seeing a sea of dead bodies drenched in blood. At the end of the hall, I see all three of them, Billy, whose broken jaw hangs askew from the rest of his face. Sandy, Nancy, and Brittany, I take a few steps forward. "I'm sorry. I'm so sorry," I say, getting down. Monster, I hear the air whisper, monster. "I'm not a monster. I didn't mean to do it. I didn't want this!" I scream. MONSTER. "Shut up!" I call, falling out of my bed onto the floor, and I crawl to the nearest corner I can find with plans to sit here till sunrise. I rush out the door as soon as they knock. "Can I have a different room?" I ask Michael, who stands beside me.

"What's wrong with this one?" He asks, patting me on my back for comfort, which I do not find, but I appreciate the effort.

"I don't know what it is about that room, but every time I go in there, my episodes are worse," I say, almost as if running out of breath. I feel as if I just ran a marathon.

"Okay, all right buddy, let's be calm here, hey breathe in" we do this simultaneously, taking a long, harsh breath. "Now let it out," we exhale. "How about we find a different room for our friend here." He says, looking at the guards who whisper to each other's ear and tell Michael there should be an expansive room just down the hall from this one. "Would this suit your fancy, Samuel?" Michael says questioningly, and I nod slowly. "All right, let me call Sharlin up here. You're going to be discussing this with her today. I, unfortunately, have another patient on one of the lower levels" he begins to walk away before I catch him by his coat.

"I think I would like that paint now," I say with a lighthearted smile.

"What sort of colors are you looking for?" Michael asks, taking out a small notepad.

"Anything you can find would be great," I smile.

"All right, let's get you down to Sharlin, shall we," he says, leading me to the meeting room. I have been sitting here for what seems like hours thinking about Brittany. Was she even real? Or was she just a figment of my imagination?

"How are you today, Samuel?" I look up to see my wife's face surrounded by the golden hair of Sharlin. Shocked by this, I lowered my head.

"I am well, I suppose," I say, hearing her take the chair from across the table. She grunts as her knees buckle into place. She shuffles around in her bag, looking for her notepad.

"That's good. How do you feel now that you have schizophrenia? Was there a time when you felt different" she says, almost as if she has something better to do? "Can you look at me, Samuel?" she asks. I do as she says, staring at her face, which has returned to its original form. "How do you feel?" she asks again, raising her right brow.

"When I was young and suffering from this, people thought I had an overactive imagination or was just overreacting. But as I grew older to what's left of the man you see before you, I felt more connected to the world around me. I even counted the ten seconds between every footstep before crushing an atom. I don't know why but everything about me just seemed alive. I noticed things that most would not. For some reason, in my last days in the outside world, I felt everything mattered, and I had never felt this before. I had always paid attention to one singular thing at a time. That semi was coming down the road. You know the rest of that story. I'm sorry if I'm rambling again" I say, rubbing my hands together.

"No, no, I think it's great. What do you think of us watching you?" Sharlin asks curiously.

"I've always had someone watching me. Ever since I was little, I was scared to be alone, so my brain put that at the forefront. A good example is when I was young, celebrating my tenth birthday, the world went dark, and I was on a swing set screaming for my mother and father to come to find me. When this vivid dream disappeared, everyone stared at me like a freak. So maybe I am." I say honestly. "Have I truly gone mad, Sharlin," I ask with nothing but curiosity carrying my voice.

"No, you just need help," she says with such confidence and conflict, I can tell she will never forgive me for scaring her that day, but I don't blame her. "Now, let us do some more of your breathing exercises, shall we," she says, taking my hands into hers. Her hands used to be soft to the touch. Now they feel as if they are fragmented and broken as if the old her has wholly vanished.

"I'm sorry for everything," I say to her with the utmost honesty one could muster forth.

"Me too," she says. I look at her curiously, "I'm sorry we couldn't get to you sooner," she says in all bitterness. "Now close your eyes," I do as she says, shutting the gates to my soul. "Breath in," we do this at the same time. "Breath out," we exhale almost simultaneously. "Now again, on your own," I take a few more slow but concise breaths. "How do you feel?" she asks. Now she is doing her job, watching as she takes a few notes.

"I feel good, for the first time in a while, I feel good," I say with a light smile. Sharlin shares this smile though I'm sure it is another falsification of Yesteryear and her many lies. She puts the notepad back into her bag.

"Good, you're free to go," she says as the metal-plated door opens. "Michael thought it would be an interesting experiment letting you walk on your own today," she says coldly, watching me with her light blue eyes. Those eyes could boil water if they wanted to. I get out of my chair and walk out into the hallway. The walk is nice without someone watching me though there is that secondhand feeling of being watched. I am sure we have all felt this, especially during the night when all the ghosts and goblins would come out of their hiding places, waiting to strike. However, most don't realize that this foreign thing could be just a tiny little kitten or a panther, depending on which side of the mountain one reaches.

On the one hand, some would reach the top and refuse to come back down. On the other, some wish never to step one foot off that mountain that is society or what's left of one. Paint buckets wait for me, five different colors, red, blue, black, yellow, and purple. The door opens, and I take two buckets in my hand and carry them into the room. I return for the other two and repeat this process once more. I look at the bed seeing a handwritten note and three paintbrushes. I go over to the side of the bed and pick each one up, feeling the bristles of each. Each can have already been left open, and now it is up to me to figure out what I will use for a muse. I dip the light paintbrush into the black bucket and cross the threshold towards the other wall; the sun flashing through the boarded-up window gives the cold room a much-needed brightness that fills my lungs. With this paintbrush, I write the story of Samuel James Dark in cursive. *Yesteryear,* I write.

I wave down the camera. Two guards come into the room. "I need a cup of water to clean my brush," I say. One of the guards retreats into the hallway and back down the corridor. "Would you like to hear a joke?" I ask the one still standing in the doorway; he shakes his head, denying the request. "At least I get a response from you," I chuckle. The man returns with a bucket full of water "thank you," I say as he sets the bucket beside the bed. Maybe this is where I belong? I think nothing lasts forever; a house has to fall at some point; it's in their nature. They leave me alone with my thoughts. "What do you think?" I ask, looking over to the window and seeing Nancy standing there admiringly. "You tell me," she says as I close my eyes, only sensing her presents. The beach is closer now, and so is the man who sits there. "Perfect," I think as the world around me grows cool with a gust of wind. "Please forgive me, my love," I say, watching as Brittany crosses over the dunes into another land, a land that someday I hope to call my own. Once I am sure I have finished for today, I lie down on the bed for a restful slumber.

CHAPTER TEN

I walk into the room, noticing that Michael is already on his side of the table. "How are we today, Samuel? Did you receive optimal rest last night?" I nod as I take my seat. "Today, we're going to play a little game. If you ask a question, I'll give you a straight answer. But, out of respect, I humbly ask that you refrain from asking me any personal questions such as my love life." He says confidently. "If you would start," he says.

"A few days ago, you said that I piqued your interest. I would like to know why?" I ask, looking above us and noticing the light no longer blinking.

"I apologize for doing this without permission, but I have read some of your stories. You are quite the poet. When studying Edger Allan Poe in high school, I always wondered what happened to this man for him to think this way. I was initially struck with curiosity, but unfortunately, I never got the chance to meet Poe. For a long time, I have been searching for someone with a similar taste for the dramatic. Once I heard about you and your story, I just had to meet you face to face and talk with you," he says. I can almost sense the excitement in his voice. "My turn. Considering we're on the topic of storytelling, I must ask what the meaning of Yesteryear is; in the past, I heard you gave it sort of a personification. You call the story by her. Why?" he asks curiously. I'll ignore the fact he asked two questions in the same sentence.

"When I wrote Yesteryear, I didn't see it as defined by words, but I suppose it's me. All on the pages are the world I live in and all the pain I feel. I gave it that personification because it made me feel close to it. In a way, it was like seeing your mother after a long day of her being away from you. I felt safe when writing Yesteryear. But, once it was finished, that safety was gone. I was so obsessed with finding my purpose that I lost everything. It cost me everything," I say as tears fall. "I killed my wife," I say sobbingly.

"Your wife?" Michael asks confusingly.

"Brittany, the woman I murdered at the hotel," I say in confusion and anger.

"Samuel, Brittany is excellent. You didn't kill her; she and the kids are waiting back home for the verdict of your trial," Michael says in aggravation.

"Then who did I murder that day?" I ask with a worried gaze.

"What are you talking about, Samuel?" Michael asks curiously.

"You said my wife was fine, did you not?" I ask in fear.

"No," he says, raising his brow. I stand up quickly. "Samuel, sit back down, please" I go over and try opening the door. "It locks automatically, Samuel," Michael says coldly, removing his reading glasses.

"Open the door," I say lightly.

"Samuel, please," Michael asks as I struggle against the door. "We will figure this out together; just give yourself some time, sit back down, and talk with me," Michael says, slowly getting up from his chair. I turn to face him.

"I said open the fucking door, Michael!" Michael stares into my eyes, showing not even an ounce of emotion.

"All right," he says as the door slowly opens. I step out into the hallway and walk back down to my room; I pick the large head paint brush and dip it into the purple and color in the bottom half of the wall below the title of the piece. I look over seeing Michael standing there in the doorway.

"I'm sorry," I say, letting the paint slowly drip down the floor.

"You have nothing to be sorry for, Samuel. We're both here to understand one another," he says, walking into the room and sitting on the bed. "Have you ever heard of the theory of normality?" I shake my head as I still face the now purple wall. "It's quite interesting normality is but a concept we as humans tend to exaggerate. There is no definitive way of describing something seen as odd or unorthodox. For example, Bigfoot or any other folk tale. When those things were first discovered, we thought they were the closest thing we could get to regarding something odd. Until more people started seeing the bigger picture and more people started seeing the same things. Then, the bigfoot started becoming more of a man, and we saw it as an everyday thing. I know you're probably wondering how this comes back to you. Samuel, unlike any I have seen or treated, you are my Edgar Allan Poe. Your mind works in such a way that only you can understand. That's a beautiful thing. It is a shame it has led you astray from what matters," Michael says with all conviction shown by a man that might care. Why should he?

"What might that be?" I ask him.

"You," he answers with a smile. "Anyway, I have bothered you for quite some time now. I would like to see that painting once you are finished," he says, walking out the door. I clean the purple paint off the brush and sit back on the bed; I forgot the ball in the other room, I think as I get up from the bed and wave down the camera. Two guards appear a few moments later, one shorter than the other.

"Last request, I forgot my ball in the other room, can you bring me a camera? I want to start recording myself. I need someone else to talk to besides you guys and the good doctors" they both nod and retreat from the doorway. I go over to the bed and pick up the notebook; this one is not like my own, it is too heavy, but it will do for now. Funny, a pin also came with it, I think, with a light chuckle. I write a new story with thoughts of her. Brittany, I think to myself as I write her perspective of our relationship. If someone listened hard enough, I am sure they could hear my thoughts.

Life: By Samuel James Dark

Why are you like this? What are you doing, my love?

Put the gavel down, and I'll come around to hug you.

I'll ask if you need help.

Why are you like this? What are you doing, my love?

Put your emotions back on the shelf, and please be better for yourself.

I'm here for you.

Take some time, gain better health, please I beg you to know your wealth.

I wish you would know when the misty mountains crumble, or the earth turns to the night sky. I will be here.

Why are you like this? What are you doing, my love?

Take your head out from the dark, and come to my side, your family and I are waiting for you.

Why did you do it? What have you done, my love?

I go down a line. Now writing from my perspective.

I'm sorry I was never there when I promised to be.

I'm sorry, we never worked. Please forgive me for taking your life on that fateful day in Yesteryear.

Maybe knowing that you are somewhere near. The beach may help me forgive myself for all the wrongs I have done.

I'll stand atop the dunes at the end of days and finally see you for all the grace that you are.

When the time comes for us to meet yet again.

We will both choose life.

I look outside the window, see the city, and cry to sleep. Thinking of all the things that have brought me here. Could there have been a way to stop this from coming? The only answer I receive is the sound of the small cricket on the cinder block which holds up this room. There is a base for this long mountain peak; I may deserve the electric chair. I have never believed in fate. I may be better off sitting in that chair. My children would be, there is no one for me to fight for besides myself. Even my ability to do that thing is minuscule. I no longer wish to live. Though I am curious about the outcome.

"Honey, I'm home," I say, arriving from the train on time; both children rush into my arms, tearing away from their Looney Tunes just to greet me. I spin them around in my arms before finally sitting them down on their feet. "How was your day, guys?" I say with such enthusiasm it's almost infectious. I kiss them both on their forehead, quickly thinking about the slander a football player received for kissing his children on the mouth. I also wonder why my mind would go there, considering that was long ago. Funny, only some things pass the test of time, unlike all those broken buildings. Then, Britany appears from the kitchen. This isn't right. I think as I walk over and give her a quick peck on the lips. I pull away quickly, seeing blood falling from her mouth.

"What's wrong, Samuel?" she asks as I look over, seeing that the television and the kids are both gone. "Are you all right ?" she asks. I look down to see the gun in my hand. I throw the gun to the side, only for it to appear back in my hand.

"I'm sorry," I say, pulling the trigger, watching as the world surrounds me in tiny flashes of fire as the bullets leave the chamber and into Brittany's stomach. She places her cold dead hand on my left cheek.

"Why did you do it? What have you done, my love?" she says as she falls to the floor, leaving a bloody handprint on my face. I awaken from this dream in a cold sweat. Knock...knock...knock the door opens without my answer, my best friend. Billy comes through the door wearing what seems to be Michael's name tag and looks healthy.

"How are you feeling today, Samuel?" he asks, writing on his clipboard. I crawl to the floor. I think you are supposed to be dead as I lower my head. "Samuel, what's wrong?" Michael says as his face changes back to its original form.

"I fear there is no help for me," I cry. "I've killed people; I didn't mean to. God or whoever is out there, please help me," I say. "End me now! Take me away from this pain! Please. I beg of you." I say as I curl myself into a little ball, looking up at Michael and seeing Sharlin stand a few feet behind him, covering her mouth as tears fall from her eyes. "I didn't want this," I say through the tears. "I don't even remember the name of my children," I say, sitting up and pressing my back against the side of the bed; I look up at the ceiling. "Please tell me. Do I even have a family? Did I teach psychology? Who am I?" I ask, fearful that I may not get an honest response. Michael walks over to me and sits down cross-legged in front of me.

"Look at me," he says softly. I do as he says. "Your name is Samuel James Dark, and you are a former psychology teacher for Lincoln highschool. You are thirty and have two children, Sarah Anna Dark and Alex Bartholemule Dark. Your wife's name was Brittany. You are waiting for your trial at the end of this month for the murders of your best friend, Billy Freeman, and his wife, Sandy Wright, formerly Mrs. Freeman, one of your students Nancy Stephens and your wife, Brittany Dark. You are currently waiting in the Lincoln Psychiatric Facility." Michael says coldly. I smile in relief.

"Thank you," I say, coming back to reality. "Help me up." He does so, helping me on my two feet. "I'm sorry about that," I say as he leads me out the door and down the hall. They let me go in first, and we have a long conversation about our lives outside the facility. Michael has a dog named Crow. I remember thinking about how fitting that name was considering his affinity with Allan Poe. Sharlin told us old tales of family get-togethers and how fun they were back in Yesteryear. I told them of my father, who wasn't there in my life. When my parents divorced, I was forced to live with my mother. I don't have any siblings that I know of. Once the session is over, they walk me back to my room and wish me goodnight. I do the same.

"Do you think we can help him?" I hear Sharlin's muffled voice through the metal doorway. Michael sighs in aggravation, "I don't know. Prescribed medication will just make it worse."

"I'm just worried that maybe once he goes back out there, he will do it all over again. Maybe he won't stop at just four. What if he takes fifteen this time around? That is what we're trying to prevent here, is it not? We're not here to be his friends, and you have more than enough patients in this facility to study. What can we fix about a man clearly losing his mind?" Sharlin asks in anger.

"Talk with him. Be there for him. That's our job; you may find a broader perspective on a hurting man once you start seeing that. I can see that you're hurting too, but my focus is on him, as should yours," Michael says, walking away. "We have to find a way to help him!" Michael says, continuing his walk. I close my eyes. The rise of the tide, the clear blue ocean. The older man sits at the base of the dunes eating what looks to be what's left of a rabbit cooked on a stick. I turn around, seeing mother earth. "Samuel," I hear Brittany say as I awaken from this dream; I look over seeing her lying on her side, propping up her head with the pillow that was always too thick for my comfort. "Nightmare?" she says, almost as if she is questioning my sanity. I lay my head back on the pillow.

"I'm not sure. *You're coming back to reality.* Billy said that the day you died. But, to be perfectly honest with you, I think I'm far from returning to that place. Reality. What is the reality of a situation if we can't understand how one feels when met with a lie such as Yesteryear," I say, draining what's left of my will down the storm drain? "Was there ever a chance for me?" I ask, not in sadness but with hope.

"There still is," she says reassuringly.

"You're supposed to say that," I say with a cold smile. "You could at least give me the truth, just this once," I say. Brittany shakes her head, denying the request. "I thought you would say that," I say as the morning sun reaches the base of the window. "You have to leave," I say.

"Will you be able to rest?" she asks.

"No, probably not," I say with no conviction. Instead, I sound like a robot, which terrifies me, though I find comfort in knowing that Brittany is staying as I turn over to get some much-needed rest.

Michael enters his office, removes his keys, and opens the mailbox. "Anything good, boys?" he asks the two guards who watch the cameras; they both claim nothing is interesting. "I wouldn't say that," Michael says with a smile as he puts the keys back into his pocket and opens the door to the mailbox. Michael takes out a Playboy magazine and sits it beside the guard on the left arm. "You know we have phones for that sort of thing now, right?" Michael says with a smile. The guard chuckles and claims he prefers the traditional way of doing things. "Oh, I bet," Michael says, sifting through the bills and coming to an unopened envelope. He takes out his keys and uses the one with the house shape to open the letter and takes out the paper. "It's too early," Michael says, looking at the report in disbelief. "Dammit!" he says, throwing the form into the trash. One of the guards turns and looks at the record. *January 13th/ time: 12:00 PM*

Verdict: Death by electrocution. Michael fixes his hair back and rubs his chin in frustration. "Two days from now," he says with a light chuckle. "Two fucking days!" he says, slamming his fist on the countertop. "Call Sharlin, tell her to get here quickly; we have to make progress, and fast," Michael says, leaving the room.

CHAPTER ELEVEN

Knock, knock, knock! Michael rushes into the room carrying his clipboard, and his coat looks like he had just grabbed it from the dirty laundry and quickly thrown it together.

"How are you feeling today, Samuel?" he asks, his face a burning shade of red; he looks over to the painting. "Are you going to finish that, or is the paint just for decoration?" he says aggravatingly; realizing this, he takes a deep breath. "Sorry, it's been one hell of a morning," he says reassuringly.

"What's going on? I have a right to know as your patient," I say demandingly.

"You are being sent to the chair two days from now," he says; winter, snow, the world surrounds itself in these things as I sit on the bed. I break out into a laughing fit. I lie on my side because of the deep pain in my stomach. I take a few controlled breaths.

"Maybe, this is my purpose, to die. I suppose this truly does answer Sharlin's question. There is no help for me." I say, holding my hand for him to shake. "I appreciate your effort, my young friend, but it all has no point now. Like myself, you two have lost your justification," I say, laughing until I cough. "No more sessions; I will accept their decision" he stares into my eyes hurtfully and stands up. He walks out the door, and I grab the paintbrush. Using every color, I paint a half portrait of myself;

on the other half of this portrait, I leave blank. I return to the bed, dropping the paintbrush onto the floor. I rip the new notebook in half, screaming away all the pain I feel, I toss the ball at the wall until my arm grows tired, and I drift off to sleep. No one is coming today as I lie in bed, thinking of what will happen tomorrow. Am I ready? No, but it is what I deserve. Today is the day. Someone slowly knocks on the door. "Come on in," I say as I slowly sit up in the bed, watching as four guards come into the room along with Sharlin, Michael, and the father of a local church. The father walks to my side and closes his hand on my shoulder.

"Do you believe in the Lord, my son?" the father asks; I shake my head. "Do you mind if I pray for you?" I shake my head once again. "Dear heavenly father, I come to you today asking that you treat this young man fairly; give him guidance, Lord, for he has lost his way. Show him your wisdom, father. Amen," he says, taking his hand off my shoulder.

"Thank you" I nod respectfully to this man. I stand up and put my arms behind my back. The handcuffs are cold and tight; I look at Michael as they lead me out the door. "I'm sorry," I say to this man I have grown to respect. "All that we see or see is but a dream within a dream," I say with a light smile. He shares this smile despite the situation.

"Edgar Allan Poe," Michael says, chuckling to himself. "I wish we could have helped you sooner," he says respectfully. "I wanted to try. Life happens." Indeed, I think to myself. I give him a respectful nod and walk up to Sharlin, who looks at me tearfully. She quickly gives me a hug. "I'm sorry for being cruel to you," she says, backing away from the hug.

"You have nothing to be sorry for," I say reassuringly as the guards take me to the elevator. "There once was this boy. His name was Sam, this boy. He had a beer bottle for a father and a lovely kitten for a mother. His relationship with the father would be none after the father met a sippy cup, the ones babies use for their apple juice." I say as the elevator doors open, and we walk forward. "The mother never met another. Therefore, she and Sam were as thick as thieves. The mother realized something about Sam; he had an overactive imagination. His brain liked to create worlds without his permission" the outside air smells clean. The sky is finally a lovely shade of blue. "These worlds would often trick Sam into believing their falsified realities" the same white van pulls up to the gate, and the guards force me inside. "Sam didn't remember his father's name, his mother, however. Her name was Lucy. She told many stories to the boy. Everything would be fine, she would tell him. Later he would call his mother Yesteryear because his mind would often look back on past lies she would sprout around the garden of truth. Lucy was her name, like seeing your mother after a long day of her being at work. Yesteryear has a way of making stories that creep their way back into view," I say as the van pulls off into the open road. I close my eyes until we stop and look out the window to see a small building; one of the guards opens the door and drags me out. I take a deep breath, and we walk up to the building. A guard opens the door, and we take a left and walk up the hallway into a darkly lit room. Any last words? The guard asks.

"Evermore," I say coldly as the door to the chamber opens, I look out the window seeing a room full of people, but none are the people I care about. No, those are all gone. Remnants of Lucy and her lies. They unlock my cuffs and sit me in the chair in the center of the room. A tear falls down my cheek. I'm sorry, Brittany. They tie down my arms and legs, tighten a strap around my chest, and place two cold objects on the side of my neck; I look out at these people seeing that they are faceless. They will see this day in black and white tomorrow. Still, they will see an image of a faceless man. There is no longer going to be living in this body. They lower the hood above my head and put the strap below my chin. The executioner goes into the other room. I take several deep breaths and close my eyes tightly as humanly possible, and the lights go out. I feel like I am falling as I walk toward the door at the back of the room. I open this door and dive into the water. Finally, I am no longer influenced by Lucy and her lies. I am brought out of Yesteryear crossing the border into a new journey where I will see my wife and children again. This I am sure of.

BOOK TWO: Sand

"When we are on beaches, we leave imprints in the sand as we take each step that gets washed away by the great tide. Life is much like a beach. The only difference to be found in the imprints a person leaves in their lives are forever long-lasting."

CHAPTER TWELVE

Brittany, I think as my body floats inside the sea. I close my eyes, afraid of what might come. Why did you have to do that, you damn fool? You have lost your family twice, have you not? Haven't you learned your lesson? I ask myself as my unconscious body surfaces, I try to move, but my body seems paralyzed to time. Finally, the tide brings me onto land that feels soft to the touch of the skin of my cheek. I no longer wish to get up but must; I open my eyes, seeing the body of sand surrounding me. I'm on a beach, I confirm to myself as I crawl into a seating position, looking up at the tall oak trees that come to an opening some miles down the shoreline. I roll up the sleeves of my white dress shirt, wondering how my clothing suddenly changed while I was drowning. Ignoring this, I jog until I notice another island in the distance, a few miles away from my own. I see a figure, a middle-aged woman, also making her way to the opening between the trees. I turn and look through the horizon of the waves rising and falling, seeing other islands located miles apart.

Where am I? I wonder as I continue with my jog. The opening leads up a small hill in the sand; I walk up this hill, reach the top and overlook the horizon. It looks as if nothing exists. A rocky trail leads over the dunes, which wave slowly like a small lake. They almost seem alive; the only thing I can see through the dark smog surrounding the trail is the ridge's end, which has also been bonded by the infernal pollution, which smells of burning wood and lost dreams. I try to go down this hill, but some invisible wall stops me. I push against this wall as hard as I can and get nowhere. Finally, my mouth falls dry, and I turn around and head back down to the water, scoop up a handful, and drink, surprised it's freshwater that tastes sweet and fulfilling. I cover my eyes and look out to the other islands finding they have vanished into thin air. I usher down the beach, struggling to catch my breath and resting my back against one of the trees. I'll need to find food soon, I think to myself as I rest in the shade of the overlooking tree, looking out into the ocean, wondering what mysteries this new land holds.

"What is this place?" I ask myself looking around and seeing nothing. Is there an end to the beach? I wonder? That is a question for another time, I say to myself as my eyes widen and I fall into slumber. I awaken to the sounds of wood burning and something cooking; I look around to see if I can catch a scent and see a figure in the distance huddling over an open flame. I get off the ground, dust myself off, and walk to this flame. The man, nothing but skin and bones and rouged-looking, cooked his rabbit on a stick. He looks up at me with his cold dead eyes, teeth jagged, and jaw visible; he flashes a menacing grin and looks back down at his food.

"So you're one of the new ones, eh?" He says in his dark grizzly voice. "Take a seat; you've had a long journey getting here. I might as well treat you to a proper dinner." He says, taking the rabbit out of the flame and reaching behind him, pulling out a sharpened rock from the brush and cutting the rabbit in fours. He has two slivers for himself and hands me the rest. "What's your name, boy?" the old man asks.

"Samuel James Dark," I say, hesitant to take a bite from the cooked rabbit, the old man practically scarfing his own. "Where are we?" I ask to take another bite. The rabbit is perfectly cooked to my liking; this man is strange and brings danger all around him. "What is this place?" I ask; he looks at me, slightly aggravated, as he finishes his rabbit.

"Best eat, boy. We've got a heavy storm coming through," he says coldly.

"But there isn't a cloud in the sky," I ask, looking up at the sky now blocked by large rain clouds. "What is this?" I ask myself; I turn to the older man finding he has vanished, leaving behind the fire and an extra four-way cut of rabbit. I eat the meal, wondering about this new place and what I left behind to get here. I haven't a clue. I can no longer remember my life in Yesteryear besides that name which eats its way into my heart every time I think of it. "Who are you?" I say, thinking of that name as I finish what's left of the rabbit and lie down for a restless slumber dreaming of a life I no longer remember living.

"Wake up!" the older man screams, causing me to jump onto my feet. "Good, you're awake. You and I are going for a little walk, Samuel Dark," he says, picking up a long stick from the weeds and leaning on it comfortably. "There is another one in there I made for you. Trust me, you'll need it knowing how far we must walk." He says, turning to a brisk walk; I wake myself up by smacking my face a few times and get the long walking stick from the weeds. I look around and see that the sands are now dark in color, and the only things left dry are the older man and me and the smoking fire. I look at the silenced flames curiously, wondering how this could be possible. "I wouldn't worry about trying to find an explanation for that, I've been here for years, and I still don't know how certain things work," the older man says a few feet away. I consider this and jog beside him, noticing all the islands are gone. "Come, we have much to do," the older man says, leading the way as we walk across the sands. "There is another like you some yards away," he says, pointing with his stick. "I believe he told me he was from Virginia. His name is Mac Slader," he says coldly. "You're probably wondering why I'm telling you this. Well, it's my job to walk up and down this beach and collect the lost people and lead them over that ridge back there," he says.

"I wasn't able to get past the border. Do you not think this would happen to Mac as well?" I ask the older man, who stops suddenly and whispers under his breath.

"Thirteen," he says coldly. "We have thirteen more to collect today. What was your question?" he asks curiously.

"How do you know the number of people here?" I ask the man; he looks up at me and grins, "Best be moving on; we're losing daylight." I'll never get a straight answer out of you, will I? I ask myself as we continue to walk forward. We walked in silence for the rest of that hour.

"There," the old man says, pointing with his walking stick. I block my eyes from the sun and look, seeing a young man huddled over, hugging himself, his long red hair bright and accurate, reflecting the sun's array. The young boy looks up at us with a worried look. "Are you here to collect me?" he asks with a broad English accent. The older man walks forward and kneels on one knee.

"That depends; are you content with your decisions in Yesteryear? Have you accepted your fate, your faults, troubles, and tribulations? Are you sure you know where to go once you reach the ridge?" The older man asks Mac; the young boy slides over and looks behind the man and me. I nod knowingly.

"Yes, I am content with my fate and the consequences behind all those wrong decisions. However, I am unsure where to go when I reach the ridge." He says worryingly; I turn, seeing another island has appeared, this one much closer to the one of which we stand than the others. I look across the body of water, seeing a woman climbing up that small hill and turning around, looking at us intently. I wave; she doesn't answer, turns around, and slowly walks out of sight. The island slowly dissipates into nothing; I turn to the older man, who seems to be watching as the young man says his silent prayers. Once finished, the older man claps him on the shoulder and gets off the ground helping the young man onto his own feet. We walk back to the opening in silence, keeping our thoughts to ourselves. It was almost noon when we finally reached the space between the trees. The older man took this boy up to the top of the hill taking his boyish young face between each hand and said something I cannot tell. The older man smiles and watches as the young boy walks down the small hill, unsure of where to go; the young boy looks around, studying the smog almost as if it were tempting him. Finally, he reaches into the pollution and falls into its tremendous gray webbing. The older man looks on in disappointment and turns to me in anger and discontent. The man rushes down the slope and stops pointing his dead finger.

"Quick rule of thumb, my friend! We never give them any direction. If they say they are content with their divisions back there, that person is content, and if they are not. Well, they aren't so lucky! Our job is to lead them here and look on as they decide between the trail and the smog. We cannot interfere. Do you understand me, boy?!" The older man screams thunderingly, the air around us crackling.

"I'm sorry, I thought," the old man cuts me off, smacking me across the face.

"Do that again, and I promise you will regret it. Even here, you have consequences Samuel Dark. When you have consequences here, the punishment is far worse than what you would receive in Yesteryear," he says, staring into my eyes with his hazardous gaze.

"Will you just explain to me what the hell even is this place!" I yell into his face, leaving tiny droplets of spit across his old tired facade.

"This is it, Samuel. This is the end of the line," he says, walking past me and dipping his feet into the calm waves. "This ocean brings in the people of Yesteryear onto the beach. Once they walk through the gates, they are brought here, where you and I lead them to the ridge and wait for them to choose whether they step into the smog or walk that trail. This is death, Samuel. All that you see around you, nothing but death," he says coldly, waving his arms around frantically. Death, I think to myself as I sit on the soft sand.

"I wasn't able to get past the wall," I say worryingly. The older man breathes an exasperated sigh as he bends into a sitting position.

"People like you and me. We won't see what's at the trail's end; we're not even allowed to traverse the smog where The Other resides. The Other is a jealous bastard, if not anything else. I wouldn't listen to a thing that man says; he does have a way of charming a man, be sure never to listen." The older man says, taking a few steps back and looking behind us. "Our next patent is this way. Sixty miles out, we will be there by daylight. There should be more along the way, another down the line, further than the rest. You are to make this journey on your own. I will collect the stragglers closer to the ridge," he says, stepping forward. I stop him grabbing his shoulder.

"Who are you?" I ask him.

"It's complicated as to who I was back in Yesteryear. Maybe I was everyone at once; my name, however, is Azrael Harris," Azrael says, flashing his broken grin. "I've never told anyone that before; it's kind of refreshing," he says as he walks down the sand. "You are coming with me," he says, looking at me over his shoulder. I exhale exhaustingly and follow after. A few hours of constant walking pass by without a word to break the silence of the wind breeze and the rising and falling of the tide, which brings forth all those sorry souls to get lost as they trail this desert of a beach. It takes us a while before we set up camp underneath some trees.

"How long have you been here, old man?" I smile as I take a bite from the perfectly cooked rabbit. The older man laughs at this remark, almost seeming ten years younger, but that look changes back to its cold dead ways after he is done with his fit of laughter.

"It's Azrael. I've been here a long time, and I'll most likely be here a long time more. I never had a life in Yesteryear. I was never gifted with that promise, so I am stuck here the same as you. I never bother trying to get past the barrier. If this is where I was put, then this is where I shall stay, and now you are here, and I don't know what that means for me." So he says, staring intensely into the burning fire as the wood cracks and breaks; this man has seen wars, men and women killing each other for decades without a word. Then, remembering the reasoning behind this question, I take the last bite from my rabbit.

"Can you tell me what my life was like in Yesteryear?" I ask the older man. He turns deep into my eyes begrudgingly, "I have to know what happened. Please." He takes a few bites from his rabbit, letting a loose piece of the meat hang from his long white beard, only clearing it off when I give my full attention to the flesh.

"I cannot reveal what has already happened or will happen. Our job doesn't work like that; no matter how much I want to help you, kid, there is no chance of you knowing what has happened. If a person remembers their life, then good for them. They died peacefully, knowing their families would be fine without them. You, Samuel, are not given the gift of knowing what has happened because what you did was wrong. What you did is best forgotten. What you did is final. There is no going back there. I'm sorry," he says, looking at me in complete remorse. "You lived and ended your life as you wished to. That was your choice; you chose that over a million choices, and for what? A pathetic search for purpose, well guess what, sweetheart? You and the other billions of people down there have none. There is no reasoning behind this!" his face glowing red with anger. "You all were born to die. That is your great purpose," he says, getting off the ground and onto his feet, dusting off his bottom. "I'm going to collect the people; you can stay or go, your choice," he says, walking away from the burning fire. His old body was being swallowed by the night air. I hear laughter somewhere behind me, I see a tall decent looking man wearing a red T-shirt and a pair of smiley-faced pajamas carrying a metal tin of what smells like burning coffee.

"So dramatic," he says, continuously laughing as he sips from the mid-shift mug. "It's funny; you still don't believe anything that old hag tells you, yet your mind is filled with scabrously apparent curiosity. I like curious people; they're easy to get to and quick to anger," he says, sitting across from me. "This is cozy," he says, warming his hands. "Do you need a snuggle over there?" he says wickedly. "I'm joking, of course. Unless you want one?" he says curiously.

"I'm okay on my own," I say with a cold stare.

"Well, the offer still stands. How long have you been here, boy?" he asks, taking a fallen stick from nearby and poking the flame, causing it to rise a smidge higher. He gasps in awe at the burning of the flame; it almost seems this man has never seen a flame before.

"I'm not so sure," I say coldly, causing him to laugh.

"You know nothing about how this land works, do you?" he asks. "Well, a day here is a year for them. So it makes the collection process quicker for your old friend who has collected at least five of the thirteen in his daily quota. He should be back shortly, but I'm not here for him; I'm here for three of those five Azzy has collected," the stranger says, propping his head up using the bottom of his right hand.

"Why?" I ask him.

"Oh dear boy, they have been awful. One has raped four children in one night. The other has committed accidental murder and killed another for just being convicted of the charges. The last is a well-known sex offender who is very boring." He says almost exhaustingly.

"Where will you take them?" I ask in curiosity, knowing I am feeding this man's ego.

"The Other. My job is to collect all the lost souls Azzy can't handle alone because of his old age, which is why you're here. You are taking his place real soon. I can feel it," he says, looking into my eyes intensely. "Ah, here they come. I can already feel one more I need to take," he says, standing up. "It's been a pleasure, Samuel. Hopefully, you and I will get along famously," he says, holding out his hand; I brush it off; he looks down at me as if I am a lesser being and walks the same way as the older man. I snuff out the flames quickly and lie down, hearing the loose waves of chatter between the older man and my newfound friend, whom I do not trust. I cannot explain to myself why I don't trust this man; there is something about him I simply do not like. I rest against the tree trunk and wait to see the older man wondering what he said before the man with the red shirt came. *"You all were born to die,"* I hear him shout, letting out his fit of anger. Is he right? Is there a reason to search for something as minimal as justification? What is my reason for being here? Why am I trapped here amongst the sand?

I'm no longer confident there is an answer to these things. Brittany, that name flashes again, running back and forth between my skull. I no longer remember what I did in my days of Yesteryear. But whatever it is, I have an immense feeling of regret. I grab a sizable fallen stick and a sharp rock and carve the stick bark off; it takes me several hours before sunrise to finally finish the blade and stick it down my pocket, which is half full of sand. I pull out the bag, clear the leftover sand, and put the knife back in my pocket. I see a large group of people walking from the horizon; Azrael is ushering forward in a brisk walk carrying his large stick.

"Are you ready?" he asks.

"I suppose," I say, looking behind him. "You've got more than you planned on?" I ask him.

"Yeah, something like that. You better get going," Azrael says as I get off the ground and dust myself off, and we go our separate ways. Azrael leads the large group to the ridge, and I go through these tiring sands.

CHAPTER THIRTEEN

The next few days were much the same, I spent most of my time walking and building new fires on this sandy wasteland filled with nothing but the dreams of Yesteryear. Lately, I have come up with a new system for myself. I collect rocks with odd colors and textures and lie them down every mile I walk to remind myself of the land from which I came. I last came back to camp a few days ago. This land seems to go on forever, much like Yesteryear; it all appears as if it is unending. There may be no end to this vast land of sand and ocean, the ocean's purest color of blue. In my pursuit, I find myself at peace because there is no company between me and the trees. I tend to think the ocean has become a bitch in its ways. I hear footsteps jogging up beside me; ignoring this, I continue to look forward and walk. Finally, the sun falls, and the world falls silent as I usher out my last few steps and set up a new campground to collect dry rocks and make a circle in the sand. After this, I go into the wooded area grunting as I push past tall leaves and low-hanging tree limbs. I collect one arm full of dry sticks and take them back to camp; even the forest at this time of night falls silent as if it were trapped in time here; I take two big leaves from one of the low-hanging tree limbs and carry my items back to the camp dropping the sticks in the center of the circle, I take the leaves and make a bowl and go over and scoop some of the fresh ocean waves which still amaze me in their realistic ways as if they and the dunes are interconnected through some great mysticism that I cannot explain with the longevity of words.

"Perfect" is the only way I can describe it, as its smooth rhythmic tones slide down a tube and rest evenly at the bottom of my stomach. I take a few more sips before crawling back to my camp and grabbing a flat rock and a thick stick; I put the base of the shaft on the rock and begin to cause friction. It takes a few minutes before a steady flame arises and sets the rest aflame; I fold my hands and warm them. I look to the night sky, seeing all the constellations and patterns of the old world; I smile and see Orion's belt, The Three Kings in some cultures, float steadily above me, knowing they will be gone by tomorrow. I take in their everlasting beauty. Brittany, I think to myself, still unknowing of what that name means. Maybe they were someone I grew fond of in my time in Yesteryear; I will never know; at least, that is what Azrael has led me to believe. I look down at the rising waves; no new islands have been seen for about a day.

Why is that? Brittany. There it is again, that name, it has to mean something; I lie down, reminded of my search for justification. Why is this the only thing withheld from my journey from Yesteryear to here? Why? I realize I have been asking that question for quite some time now and still find myself without an answer. The older man tells me as he wishes, and the man in red tells me his pathetic lies to keep himself out of trouble and out of The Other. I have yet to find out his name. I no longer wish to find out, I tell myself as I lie down, propping my head up using my forearms.

My eyes fluctuate until I fall asleep. I dream of me and another driving down what seems like a freeway going over the speed limit. The red truck was almost filled with blood as I heard the screams of what appeared to be children looking in through the window and seeing a dead body. I woke in a heated sweat, curious about what the dream meant. I get off the sand and watch the morning sunrise as a new island appears a few miles away from my own. I wonder if there are others like Azrael and me. Perhaps they already know where they will go when they reach the ridge. This is a question I should ask later, I say to myself as I leave behind the flat rock and kill the flame to a burning halt. I continue walking until I see a figure lying down in the sand some distance away; from this distance, it seems to be a young boy, maybe who has had a birthday recently. I rush up to the body, pull him out of the current, and flip him onto his back; I lightly smack him three times and pump him down on his chest. He wakes in fear jumping and writing as the water jumps from his throat, he coughs for a long time before settling down and resting in the sand. I look at this boy with kindness. The boy sits up and looks at me in remorse.

"Where am I?" the boy asks, looking at the world around him curiously, only to find himself even more confused. This boy is me.

"That my boy gets complicated. You see this sand," I say, picking up a handful and letting it slowly slither from my fingers. "All of this and the islands you will grow to see as a constant is all a part of your journey over the ridge, which is back that way," I say, pointing to the sands leading the way I have come. "I have traveled far for you just to lead you back home again. Quite redundant when you think about it, isn't it?" I ask with a smile, trying to keep this young man's experience light-hearted. "What do you remember?" I ask him, sitting cross-legged.

"We had a school trip to the Empire State Building (the new one being rebuilt). They hadn't put the safety gates up yet on the top of the edge of the building, and my friends dared me to get up on the edge and attempt to walk across to the other end, and I fell. I'm not sure of what happened next." I thought someone remembering their lives in Yesteryear was impossible; why does this boy remember his death with such vivid detail? I question myself looking into the boys' light green eyes as they search for the windows to my soul.

"What is your name, mister?" the boy asks me.

"Samuel Dark, I'm your guide to the ridge; I am not permitted to cross it with you, however," I answer the boy, feeling a sharp burn fly across my temple. Ignoring this, I focus on the boy. "What is yours?" I ask the child.

"Wayne Gilbert," he says; I nod.

"Before returning to the ridge, I must ask you some questions. Are you okay with that?" he does not give me an answer but looks to the islands that appear and dissipate. "You will learn to get used to that the further we travel," I say, clapping my hands together; the boy practically jumps from his skin and looks up at me, giving his undivided attention. "Are you content with your life in Yesteryear? Have you made peace with your decisions, and are you willing to answer for your wrongdoings?" I look down at this young man waiting for what seems like hours for him to contemplate his answer. However, I am not bothered by this, so I wait patiently.

"I guess I don't understand the question," the boy says questioningly. I stand up, dust myself off, help the boy onto his own two feet, and dust him off using my walking stick.

"You will," I say, walking down the handmade path and listening as the boy follows. I look up and see storm clouds as the sun sets at noon. The older man said I am slowly getting used to this place and only being here for two days or two years.

"We should set up camp soon," I say as a wave of rainfall comes crashing from the sky, screaming as it hits the sands. The tides rise and fall steadily unbeknownst to the storm above; I suppose the ocean is taking this kindly today, I think, chuckling at the thought of the waves being alive. I remind myself as we walk up to two trees, their leaves piling on one another, blocking us from the rain. "This is as good a spot as any!" I yell behind me as I sit, resting my back against one of the trees. The boy does the same; he seems to be holding himself together reasonably well considering all that's been revealed, I think to myself. I look at the young man in curiosity. "Tell me something, young man" he looks up at me. "What is the future like?" I ask curiously. He looks as if surprised.

"What do you mean!?" Wayne asks, yelling his question through the rainfall.

"I came here during a time long forgotten. I wonder if anything has changed over time," I say with a light-hearted smile, thinking of the ridiculousness of having a conversation about a time I never got to see but can still learn from. Wayne tells me things I would never consider; the world is similar to how it was left when I came to the sands. Their school systems now teach them things such as the second Cold War, which caused the fall of the original Empire State Building, a widespread power outage that would take out most of America, and the assassination of a President and the Vice President on the same day. They would also teach about the Apollo Space landing and consider it a conspiracy to promote our government which I find far-fetched. It takes the boy nearly an hour to tell me all he has learned from Yesteryear, enthused in talking to someone from 2022.

"What was your life like," Wayne asks me curiously, the rain now silenced to mere droplets, mist hanging over the land blocking the view of any potential islands to appear. I look out into the fog and think of that name and how beautiful it sounds, running circles around my brain. Brittany, I am sorry for any wrong I dealt you.

"I can't say. I can only remember bits and pieces of what my life was like; the older man revealed to me that people like him and I don't get to remember our lives if we are fortunate enough to have one, of course," I say, almost admitting to defeat, I may never find my purpose in this place, I may never get the justification I so desperately long for.

"What can you remember?" Wayne asks as he lies flat on his back, facing away from me.

"I remember a name and a terrible accident that would define me in my last days. The name belongs to a woman, and I love her dearly. So why did I come here? Why did I leave such a beautiful name behind to defend herself?" I ask myself looking down at my new friend; this friendship will never last. I accept that despite not having anyone else to talk to besides the older man and the man from The Other, even though they are not very fond of company, it is good to have someone that comes from my land and is just as confused about their surroundings as myself, I close my eyes in hopes there are more like he and I so I won't feel so lonely here. I received a restful sleep that night, which I have not had for quite some time now. I dream of that name, Brittany, and the two children we have together, the little girl growing up to become the spitting image of her mother and my son taking my likeness. I reach out to them and find myself stuck; a wall is standing in my way; who are these people? I think as the little boy shakes me, pleading for me to wake up. I open my eyes to the calm orange morning sky with hints of pink floating about, calmness replacing irritation. I sit up and watch as the stars leave my sight. I look over at Wayne, who sits steadily, waiting for my word.

"Are you ready to eat?" I ask him picking up my walking stick and stepping one foot into the weeds.

"Yes, please," he answers. I nod and walk into the weeds, determined to find food for the both of us; I walk over the leaves at a steady and slow pace; I hear a sound rustling through the thicket of the weeds.

I stand still and wait for the world to once again fall into motion; a rabbit big enough for one person crawls its way out of the base of the weeds shaking off dirt leftover from its wiery travels. I lift the stick above my head and stab it into the rabbit's head, cutting it clean off, its back leg thumping around before coming to a halt. I pick up the rabbit's body, carefully remove what's left of its head from the body, and throw the remains into the thickened weeds.

"I'm sorry, my furry friend," I say to the body as I carry it back to our camp; I tell the boy to look away as I skin the dead animal and cook it over a large flame bringing it to a steady sear. I cut the body down the middle, removed the innards for the boy and me, and threw them into the thicket. I sit on his side of the rabbit on a flat stone and call for the boy; he comes and eats his meal hurryingly. I eat half of mine before letting him finish it off for me. After he has finished, I walk over to the body of water, scoop a handful into my hands, and pour it onto the flames. The twigs grow red hot until they settle into pure darkness.

"We better keep moving," I say, helping the boy onto his feet. "We've got a lot of land to cover," I say, letting him lead the way down the long stretch of beach. "We should be halfway there by nightfall," I say, ruffling the boy's bright red hair.

"Why do I have to go over the ridge?" the little boy asks.

"So you can go home, wherever that is," I say hesitantly.

"Heaven?" the boy says curiously.

"Possibly, if you believe in that sort of thing, I wouldn't know. But, if I had to guess, what's over that ridge is something you can only think of with your imagination," I say confidently.

"That's an interesting way of seeing it," he says enthusiastically. I laugh lightly.

"Yes, I suppose it is," I say. We both fall silent as we continue to walk down this grueling beach; the boy looks around in awe at the world around him, being sure to take every little detail, noting the softness of the sand and the clean air as it swims through his lungs, I admire his sense of wonder and joy knowing what it means to go over that ridge. I sometimes wish I had shared this sense of wonder and blissful happiness. So perfect. I smile as we continue to walk down the beach in higher spirits.

We reached the halfway point by nightfall and set up our camp, the boy sitting in front of me warming his hands against the fumes of the flame.

"We learned about something like this place back home," the boy says lightly. I look over the burning brush and motion for him to explain further. "One of my teachers asked us one day, *What do you think happens after death?* Which to me is a very odd thing to ask but the teacher was a very odd person. Some gave answers such as Heaven or eternal darkness, the teacher would tell all of us were wrong, and she would tell us that *Death is how the person dying perceives it.* I thought that was very interesting, considering you said something similar earlier," the boy says.

"Everything around us is caused by perspective. How we see the world around us is different from another. For example, say you see a world of color, and another would see the world as broken and unhinged," I say to the boy.

"How do you see the world, Sam?" he asks.

"Lost," I answer. We sit there for an hour in silence until Wayne decides to lie down and fall asleep. I wait a few moments watching the boy toss and turn to dream of something dreadful and fearsome. In this life, we are all lost in our self-centered ways, I think to myself as I lie down and fall into the world of dreams. The front of the tomb has nothing, not a name, birth date, or date of death. It's just an open door. I remember this door but not its meaning. That man; is this his tomb? I wonder, looking at the area and noticing the woods which surround the grave and the visitor in a stalkerish way as if the trees are on the hunt looking for prey.

I look down at the tomb and see one name and nothing else: **Samuel J. Dark,** the scribe read, fainting into existence the quote Brittany had left. How do I know she left this? **Goodbye Yesteryear** below that: **Goodbye Starry Night Sky** I get down onto one knee, running my index finger over each letter and its curvature. I wake up to the morning sun, the boy still sleeping soundlessly; I get up, making sure not to wake the boy, and walk down to the ocean, where the water covers my feet. I stand here, letting the wind a fresh, bright breeze against my face. Why did you have to leave your family? I ask myself, All that pain you must have caused her, and for what? Justification, a reason for living? Why didn't you fight for your life, you damn fool!?

"I'm a fool," I say to myself, searching for any sign of solace as memories of my time in Yesteryear bring themselves forward; the last thing I can remember entirely was my death. The static electricity pushes and pulls through my skull as my world falls into a blinding light; I remember the people watching me die behind that window. They were all faceless, which terrifies me dearly. "You are a damn fool," I tell myself as I open my eyes, waves still pushing against the bottom half of my legs as small fish swim around them in a circular motion. I chuckle as they attempt to take little bites out of my legs. Finally, I usher the child through the waves back to the child, I shake him until he awakens, and he sits up and stretches out before getting onto his feet "Is it time to go?" he asks, looking up at me.

"Yes, it's time for you to meet a new friend," I say, patting him on the head and leading him down the homemade path of rocks. Yesteryear has a name. I think it was the same as my mother's. Lucy would often lie about things getting better; they never did, however.

CHAPTER FOURTEEN

"I have finally remembered my time in Yesteryear," I say, looking down at the boy as a silhouette of a tired old figure comes into view. "I was an unhappy man though I cannot imagine why; I had it all back then, and yet I was filled with so much pain, I killed four people, a friend, a widow. One of my students and my love, Brittany. I do not know the reason why I did these things. Then, I was a sad man, and now I feel nothing besides guilt for what I have done to those who trusted me the most. I have done terrible things, and I know that now, though I am not yet certain why I am not allowed to cross into The Other despite all my wrongs. I'm not quite sure what my place here is," I say; the boy looks down, contemplating.

"Maybe it's your job to find out. Maybe here you will find the peace you were searching for Yesteryear. Instead, you sought justification, yet you don't realize why you are truly here," the boy says coldly.

"Yes, I suppose it is, young man; what do you think of when you hear the word Life?" I ask him as the older man scurries towards us; surprisingly, the boy seems unfrightened by this man. He almost seems comfortable seeing this man and his deadly stare as he walks across the same beach.

"I don't know; what do you think of it?" the boy asks. I chuckle, thinking this is a mere boy standing beside me. Yet, I still treat him as an equal, as all adults should with the youth of Yesteryear.

"I think of trees and how they move when hit with a powerful enough wind. I think of the ocean and its cool full blue beauty as it goes along with itself-maid currents. I think of every living thing all at once being united as one. I also think of the pain we endured to get to that beauty. I sometimes think of the odd statement that *all men and women are created equal,* yet we never treat each other as such. Your experiences are not the same as my own, but we still hopefully have great respect for one another. I sometimes wonder if Yesteryear is truly doomed to live in an endless cycle of pain only to find itself tasting the sweet supple aroma that is peace. I may never know why I belong here, lost amongst these great planes we call the sands, which seem never-ending. Though, for some reason, I hope I will never have to cross over the dunes. I think I don't deserve a choice between the two. I never knew it would end like this for me." I say, carrying pain and heartbreak in my voice as I look out past the rising tides watching as new sands come and dissipate into nothing, forever lost just like Azrael and me

"Can I ask you something?" the boy says questioningly.

"Of course, we still have a little time," I say, watching as the old man continues to walk forward and stops halfway as we reach closer to one another.

"Do I have to go over the ridge?" the boy asks.

"Yes, but if you would like, I can walk you as far as I can up the ridge," I say, smiling down at the boy, taking him by the shoulders.

"I would like that," he says. I lead him to the foot of the hill and nod to Azrael respectfully and walk up the mountain with the boy. We both look out into the horizon taking in the dark cloud that is the smog. The boy grows cold and hesitant with each step he takes as he walks down this hill, which I am not allowed to cross. Finally, the boy looks behind him up to me and waves goodbye. I share this embrace and watch as his body disappears over the horizon. Finally, I smile to myself and walk back down the hill.

"How did you get along?" the old man asks.

"Famously," I say.

"Good, that should be all for today anyways. Have you already eaten?" Azrael asks. I nod. "Good, take the rest of the day to yourself; I need to discuss a few more things with the men from The Other and The Beyond, nothing too concerning. We're just going to discuss your place here in this land," he says as if answering a question I have not asked.

"Why would you need to discuss me and my place here?" I ask him.

"Ask no questions, and I will tell you no lies," he says, walking past me. "You will find your answer soon enough; perhaps you will know when I return. Over the next two days, I would like you to walk along this beach and meditate to yourself since the presence of others wanders like drunken harlots throughout this mass of land. So you should expect three tomorrow and one the next. Consider yourself lucky," the older man says, walking into the brush of weeds.

"How do I know where to look?!" I call. I wait for a few moments standing here as if I am a statue watching the city destroy itself around me, the world forever moving on without me to bother much of anything; I receive no answer to this question. "I guess it's up to me to figure it out for myself," I tell myself as I walk up to the tree line and sit under a tree with the perfect shade hidden from the sun. I grab a loose stick behind me and draw a frowning face into the sand. "Why so sad?" I ask this face as I whip the canvas clean leaving only fragments of what was, such as life, I think to myself. Next, I draw what I think of as buildings, each one taller than the last. Next, I draw spirals above what I assume to be an eastern European town in the dead of night; the only thing I can genuinely have again is the feeling that painting gives me when I look back at it. The

Starry Night. The perfection that is the human mind in all its strange ways reminds me of this painting.

"Nice drawing," the man from The Other's voice says, coming out of the weed brush. "Really heartfelt," he says, sitting beside me; I move over. "You can call me Azazel, by the way, though I go by many names. The reason why I am trapped here is far different from the older man. I was brought here by force because I thought the world needed a bit of pain and war. I defied the man from The Beyond, so he sent me to The Other, where its corruption ruined my original appearance. I can keep this form, but for only a limited time. After it is gone, I revert to my demonic state in which I undergo an eternal existence in pain. I have fallen," he says, laughing to himself. "Your people would make goat sacrifices to me because they thought it would appease me. They were wrong, of course; nothing ever would please me. I was arrogant, and now I think I have grown immensely. I hate that old man with every fiber in my being. He has always been a favorite of the man from The Beyond. Now you are here to replace the old man slowly deteriorating with age. He will be gone soon. I suppose I just wanted you to know that" he gets back onto his feet. "You are going to be trapped here for a long time, my young friend," he says, walking back into the weeds. I look to the ocean, wondering how this world truly works. Just who is this man who resides in the land of The Beyond? What is really at the end of that trial? I ask myself these questions until nightfall, when I would receive little but peaceful sleep. In this dream, I stand before a tall mirror, my reflection looking at me with his cold empty husk of a face; I hold my hand out and touch this mirror, trying to get to this faceless man who seems almost troubled because of his deformities. "What has happened to us?" the man in the mirror asks. "Why have we caused so much pain to the loved ones?" he asks. I look at him in a powerful wave of remorse. "I don't know," I say. The reflection backs away from the mirror and looks at me angrily, his face showing that anger by scrunching together. "You killed her!" he screams.

"I know!" I cry out as I fall to my knees, covering my face from the view of the man with no face. "I wish I could change that. I wish I could change everything." I say, looking up at my reflection, which seems to follow my every move, my face finally appearing in this terrible lie. Finally, I wake up, wash my hair in the ocean, and let it air dry as I sit in the sun. I close my eyes and breathe slowly, taking in the scent of the flowing sea and the wind blowing to the east. I feel a wave rush over me, filled with adrenaline, as visions of the people I am supposed to collect come forth. One was an older woman far beyond the ridge to the left part of this island, and a man carrying his son walks forward into view, and the vision fades away. I blink a few times before I am brought back to this strange new version of reality. I walk back up the beach, collect my walking stick, and usher forward, walking on the scolding hot sands.

"Hello, friends!" I call out to the figures walking in the opposite direction, and the two tallest figures turn and face me. I rush forward and hold out my hand once the man of the group is close enough. "Welcome to The Sands. It's a beautiful land of great mysticism. I am Samuel, your guide to what you believe to be an eternity. You all look tired, so we will camp here for the night and go the other way. Is your boy there feeling well?" I ask the man.

"He's fine," the man says coldly. The woman reaches out and clutches my left hand between her own "Are you here to help us?" the woman asks.

"I am," I say as I lead them underneath some trees. I take three large leaves from the trees that hang above and go over to the body of water, taking three cups full of that clean water and taking it back to the group. "Drink up. We have a long journey tomorrow," I say, looking into each of their eyes, the man filled with anger and remorse, much like myself in Yesteryear. The woman is exhausted and terrified, and the boy looks like he has caught a bad cold on his journey as he lies in the soft sand. I lean over and take his head into my hands. The man stops me, and I look up at the man. "This will keep him hydrated. I can't explain how. You will have to trust me just this once." The man nods, agreeing.

"Thank you," he says silently. I give the boy the water and help him by lifting the cup to his blusterous mouth.

"Good?" I question with a smile. The boy looks up at me and smiles as he fades into a deep sleep. "He will make it out of this bouncing and screaming soon enough," I say to the man.

"How are you so sure?" the man asks neglectfully.

"I just know. If I have learned anything during my time here, there is always some solace with how things turn out for those who truly think they can reach whatever is on the other side of that door." I smile, giving him and the woman there leaves full of water. "Now drink and rest," I say. They do as I say and finish their waters almost as quickly as I gave them.

"Are you an angel?" the woman asks through her sips. I chuckle at the thought.

"I am not. I don't deserve that title; I'm just a simple person like yourself willing to give you the kindness that Yesteryear would not. I am nothing but a simple guide to that great plane of which is still a great mystery to me," So I say as I consider the actions I have made in Yesteryear; I find myself accepting my fate back then, and there is nothing I could do or say to change my destiny. "You will find that this land holds great beauty, but for now, you all must rest" I smile, and the man and the woman lie down and fall to a peaceful slumber. I get up and walk away from the group of people and head to the ocean, which is excellent against the hairs of my legs. "I'm sorry, Brittany," I say, looking out as the sun sets behind the rising and falling of the horizon. I walk back up the beach and lie a few feet away from this small group. I stayed this way for hours, staring at the night sky in a daze, thinking of my life if I hadn't pressed that pen's button. *Click* went Lucy and her lies. *Click* went to the old world and her promises of a better world. What a fool I was, I think to myself as my eyes begin to rise and fall. You're trapped here. Are you prepared to live with that?

"I am," I say as I sleep, dreaming of a peaceful dream. Finally, I wake up in bright spirits and watch the group huddled over a self-made fire. I walk over, sit on the opposite end of the flame, and lean over to the child. "How are you feeling, young man?" I ask softly. The boy looks up at me, smiling brightly.

"I'll be okay," he says sickly. You have a long way to go before you are okay, my young friend, but I appreciate your spirit and drive to move forward. So I think, showing my admiration through my movement by ruffling his long curly brown hair. "May I ask your names?" I tell the group of people, Mary, a beautiful young woman wearing a short white dress ripped at the bottom and a pair of black All-Stars. Kory is a middle-aged man wearing a green T-shirt and brown boots of a brand I do not recognize. Drake, the young boy wearing a black and white striped shirt and blue jeans (typical children's attire), Mary looks up at me questioningly.

"What is your name?" the woman asks.

"Samuel Dark, I was once a high school teacher who lost his way, and now I'm trapped here leading other lost folks to their end. Whatever that looks like, I will never know. What did you do back in Yesteryear? What were your professions?" I ask curiously.

"I did accounting work," the man says. I laugh at this.

"After all these years being stuck here, they still cannot find a way to make the robots do the work for you," I say with a bright smile causing the man to chuckle.

"Some things require the imperfections of the human touch." He says lightly, removing his cold stature and replacing it with a warm, open feeling. "What about you?" the man asks the young woman.

"I was a college tutor going for a graphic arts major," she says confidently.

"That's very interesting. May I ask you both a question?" both agree. "What do you think of when you hear the word Life?" So I ask both of them, and they look at each other and ponder this question for quite some time.

"I think of my family and all the good times we had. But I also think of the troubles and tribulations we had to fight through, all the pain we had to suffer just to get to the point of having those good times," the woman says. I nod, taking in this answer; I look at the man and wait for him to answer.

"I think of my son and how much time we spent together. Once you have children, they make your life worth living. Their minds are so complex and creative in so many ways I often wish I still carried that large of an imagination." The man says, smiling and ruffling his son's hair. I wince at this, thinking of my children and the time I have missed in their lives. I missed their weddings, graduations, and the most critical years of their lives. I began to cry, and they both looked at me questioningly. I missed so much time, and now they are dead. They have journeyed over the ridge through the gate I cannot travel past. I get onto my feet and look at the sick boy. He can make it if the man can carry him the rest of the way without stopping. I think to myself.

"We better get moving," I say coldly, walking towards the land of the ridge, the woman quickly following after without question. The man does the same, picking up his son and carrying him like a husband does his wife when they first married. Brittany, I think to myself, remembering our wedding. Why you damn fool? Why did you have to kill them all?

Wanting to feel something is no longer a plausible enough answer, is it? You had it all, you damn fool! So I think to myself, continuing to walk at a hurried pace.

"Can you slow down?" the woman asks as if she were tired. I ignore her.

"Hey, jackass, slow down!" the man screams a mile behind me. I turn to see them both following closely after. "What the hell was that all about?!" the man says, raising his voice.

"You both had such fulfilling lives. I killed the ones who were there for me. Before that, I was hurting and still am because of what I did! I relive every moment almost every second of the day, trying and trying to change my mistakes only to find out they are permanent. You and your boy had more time together than I would ever have with my children! How is that fair? You were happy! What do I get? A twenty-five hundred voltage battery, ramping its way through my skull!" I say, filled with bitterness and the loss of heart. "I was never happy, though. I had a good wife and a fucking family. I had to take that away from myself because I was searching for something I still haven't found an answer to," I say, turning to the crashing waves.

"I wasn't happy. I was an addict. I took too many pills, my boy," he stops taking a sharp breath, wrapping his hand around his son's shoulder. "He entered the living room and found me dead, looking up at the ceiling. When you're a child, you get curious," he says, looking down at his son's cold empty face.

"So he took too many," I say coldly, looking down at the boy.

"I blame myself, not only for my life but also for my ignorance. This boy will never see his mother again until she comes to this strange place. Sure, we were happy once, but we ended that life of happiness with pain." He says, walking past me; I look after him as he slowly walks the sand.

The woman claps me on the shoulder, looks up in admiration, and walks after the man and his child. I follow after her.

"So what is this place?" the woman asks as I approach her.

"As far as I'm concerned, it's neither life nor death. It's that fine line between the two: these sands are alive, like the ocean. It somehow speaks only in whispers. First, all of you will face The Other, that place I know nothing about, and I cannot tell you which direction you should take. I can only lead you to the doorsteps. After that, it's your choice as to where that road will lead you," I tell the woman. "I will only help you to a certain point in this place. The foot of the ridge is where we shall part ways," I say coldly.

"What will happen to you?" she asks.

"I will wait for the next person to come over the great tide, and similarly, I will lead them to the ridge and ask them to depart. However, if they do not wish to leave, I will allow them to stay until they are ready," I said remorsefully.

"What if we are not ready," she asks as we get ever so closer to the ridge and its promises of a better world over that edge. I look at her in confidence.

"You are ready. Are you content with your choices in Yesteryear and the consequences of those choices? Are you aware of who you are and who you were? Have you come to terms with knowing your fate while here?" I ask her.

"I am," she says, unsure of herself.

"Then you are ready," I say as we walk up to the foot of the ridge, where the man and his child wait for me to say something. "I am sorry for what I said earlier, it was foolish, and I hope it has not botched your decision when you go over that ridge," I say, pointing at the dune.

"Don't worry about it," the man says. I don't believe him, but I appreciate the attempt.

CHAPTER FIFTEEN

The man had left his child for The Other. The young woman takes the child in her arms and carries the child to The Beyond. I smile at seeing this great act of heroism saving the boy because his mind is still pure and full of love and imagination. I feel as if I helped this boy, even if it was in a minuscule way. I felt good about myself for the first time in a long time. Good. I felt perfect with all my imperfections. I know it cannot last, and I am okay with that realization. So I think to myself as I walk back down the opposite way, back to the sands and their bright aura, which tell no truths and hold the most mysterious of lies. I stand before the ocean current, take a long hard breath, close my eyes, and think of Yesteryear, the story untold. I imagine the last few words in that story bright as day:

What is value? Is it what one is worth, or is it simply another lie Yesteryear tells us when we are young and full of color? This question may never be answered with the utmost honesty, but I have told you my tale. I have shared my story, yet I feel indifferent about the ending. There still seems not to be one in sight. I grab my new pen.

CLICK… went to the old world… CLICK went Yesteryear and her lies of a better world. After all, this is done. After a story's end, perhaps I will find value elsewhere. Maybe I will finally wear that smile once again. Onto you, I give my account to do with as you wish. I have no reason to worry anymore. I am free to roam the stars like the ones before me. I wonder what life is like after Yesteryear. Maybe there is nothing. My heart is open to infinite possibilities as my spirit leaves descending into that shallow light. Finally, I will be happy once more.

Way back in Yesteryear.

"Finally," I frown, remembering my last word on the day of my death. Evermore, I think to myself. "I was never truly happy in the first place, and now I am burdened with this undying guilt of all the things I had done" I remember crashing Thomas's truck into the motel sign. I remember the look on Nancy's face when I said those horrible things. I remember cutting her throat open. Why? So much pain for nothing, and yet life is pain and beauty all at once though beauty should never be searched for while in pain. I wish I had realized this sooner. I look past the ocean and see a body floating in the restful seas. Azrael never said anything about a fourth person coming to shore? I say to myself, questioning the appearance of whom I assume to be a black male floating in the water as if forever submerged. The waves flow as silence fills the air. I go over and pull this man onto the shore. I see six more islands, each with a large group of ten people wandering about.

"He did it," Azrael says worryingly, appearing behind me. "He allowed another war," he says, returning to the ridge. "Are you happy with this, Ariel? You are supposed to protect them, you bastard! Look at all this bloodshed. It doesn't look like you are protecting much of anything," he retorts, turning his back to me. I turn to see a tall figure standing atop the ridge.

"I protect the gates of The Beyond. You know that I cannot interfere with their choices. I can only open the door now, do your job and lead them here!" the figure says, turning his back away from us.

"Damn you," the old man says angrily "you take this beach, and I'll take the rest," he says, walking away. I go to stop him though I cannot move. I stand here looking on with worry as he walks and walks, counting each second it takes for his foot to hit the ground. I kneel and pump on the man's chest until he rises and spits out a pool of water. He looks at me confusingly.

"Who are you?" the man asks.

"I am Samuel, your guide to The Beyond," I say with a bright smile looking on as the islands begin to disappear. "You need to tell me if you are content with your decisions in Yesteryear and do you accept the consequences of those decisions?" I say in contempt.

"What does that mean?" the man asks. I look at him curiously.

"What does what mean?" I ask.

"Yesteryear" I look at him for a long moment and stand up straight, holding my hand. "I will tell you if you walk with me," I say, hesitant. The man takes my hand, and I help him onto his feet and walk him underneath the overbearing trees. I sit down, pressing my back against the wood of one of the tallest trees in the litter. He does the same sitting beside me. Finally, I turn to look this man in the eye.

"The answer is quite simple, and yet the meaning behind the word strays far from its actual meaning, which you would find in a dictionary. It is also far beyond the stories it can tell. In my prediction, Yesteryear is not a time or place. It is not described in simple words. To me, it is undefined, especially when compared to the mysteries these sands hold and the memories Yesteryear tends to keep hidden from us. My Yesteryear is my mother, Lucy though she has no connection to this place. The Sands are simply the end of Yesteryear, meaning life. Yesteryear is not defined by one thing. It can be whatever you wish for it to be. I am here to lead you to the road which goes to The Beyond. You can assume what you wish about what lies in The Beyond. I do warn you, although I am not permitted. Stay far away from The Other. Its temptations are deathly, as is the one who resides there, Azazel, a real bastard if I have ever seen one," I say coldly. The man looks out into the weaving seas and ponders what I have revealed.

"Why God; why now?" he says to himself.

"I do not believe God has anything to do with this place, I have only seen three others that come here often, and the third I just met a few moments ago. You two will be more acquainted if you decide to follow the path. One has been a decent friend of mine over the past few days. His name is Azrael. I think he has plans to leave me behind in this place, and I'm fine with that. I quite like it here." I said, laughing to myself as the man left for the ridge. "I hope you find peace, wherever that may take you," I call after him as I watch the rest of the islands dissipate. It took Azrael a long time to finish his tasks; by the time he returned to camp, it had already struck nightfall. So now we sit here in silence, watching the fire burn and crackle as two squirrels cook over the flame.

"I'm sorry for not being very present as of late," he says, blowing off excess smoke from the fried animal.

"Don't worry about it. I like to think I handled myself very well?" I say as I take mine out of the flame and stick the but of the stem into the ground, letting my animal cool off; Azrael takes a large bite out of his own.

"You know what I like most about squirrel meat? It's almost soft and chewy like a piece of bubble gum," Azrael says, chuckling through his bite, chunks of the animal's flesh flying out of his mouth into the open flame. "Ariel is nothing but a blowhard. He tries too much to please the man from The Beyond. I realized several years ago that nothing will please that man," he says as he takes another bite. I work up the courage to take a bite from my own. "You made a mistake again today. I know you did," he says, looking deeply into the flame. "The Beyonder blames me, so you will be replacing me tomorrow. Permanently," he says coolly.

"I didn't realize I had made a mistake. I'm sorry." Azrael shrugs this off.

"It had to happen, eventually. I'm old and withered. I fear my time is almost up anyways," Azrael says, chuckling and breaking into tears. "You know I'm going to miss this place. Everything about it, even the people who wonder about it, I'll miss them too. I've made it. I might be the only one to make it. But I don't want to go, honestly. This place holds all my fondest memories and all the pain I have been through. This place is my home, and now it is being taken from me by the most capable person to take care of it. Promise me you will take care of this place for as long as you have it," he says, dropping his food into the flame. "I need to know before I go," he says with a relaxed smile. I take my last bite from the animal and toss it into the flame. We watch the piece curl into a tight ball and disintegrate into the fire.

"I promise," I say as tears trickle down my cheek.

"Good. That's good," Azrael says, closing his eyes as his body breaks apart and flows with the wind, leaving only the imprint in the sand where he sat down. I wonder as his remains float into the sky, creating new stars and constellations.

"Amazing, isn't it." I jump to the man's voice. I look around, noticing a dark figure holding his hand up as if surrendering to something. "Nothing to fear, I am but a weary traveler such as yourself," the man says, coming into view; this man wears an all-white robe.

"I assume you're The Beyonder?" I ask this man. He chuckles as he sits across from me and warms his hands over the flame. "You're the one who decided the old man should go, not me. Why is that?" I ask this man.

"Azrael deserves to rest. He has spent years in this place looking on as the world destroys itself, leaving him with nothing to do about it. In a way, he needed to leave. He had grown old and tired, he was one of my closest friends, and now he can rest easy knowing you are here to take the reins, as they say. I have a reason for everything, my young friend. You just need to trust me," The Beyonder says with a heart-warming smile. "I came here to warn you before I decide on anything further. I am planning a cataclysm that will destroy not only all life on earth but the entire universe," he says, looking closely into the flame.

"Why?" I ask him.

"When the day comes, I will reveal all the truth you so seek," The Beyonder says, standing back up and reaching for my hand. "It was a pleasure to meet you, Samuel. I will be coming here to check on you every other day," he says before returning to me. "I know you must think less of me now, but I promise, I do everything with love," he says as he traverses up that little hill. With love, I laugh as I watch the flame burn ever brighter.

"I see you've heard about the old man," Azazel says, coming out of the tall weeds. I look up at him and motion for him to take a seat, and he does so with a slow hesitation. "The same will happen to me once The Beyonder says so," he says, almost as if he is afraid. "I know he and I have had our differences in the past. But I don't want to die," he says, pleadingly looking at me over the flame. I lean forward to warm my hands, the night is cool and crisp, and it feels like it has plans to snow.

"It's fucked up. At the end of our term, it all falls down to The Beyonder's final choice of where you're going, The Beyond, The Other, or The Dark. As far as I know, there isn't a point in trying to stop it from happening. There is no reasoning with fate; that's the golden rule," he says. I have never felt such anger from Azazel, not quite like this.

"What happens after people like you and Azrael die?" I ask as I look up at the sky, remembering the new constellations.

"Some are fortunate to see The Beyond; others like him and me," he points to the sky. "We're not so lucky. When it comes to Yesteryear, you get a chance to improve things. Here, you get one try, and after you fail. After that, you're done for, that's why we have been in this place for so long. We have never made a mistake. Until he did," he says, looking back up to the stars. "You old damn fool," he says lightly.

"It wasn't him who made a mistake," I say coldly.

"You?" I nod my head. Azazel looks away dismissively and turns back to me "how many times have you made this mistake?" he asks angrily.

"Twice," I say, remembering the colored man and the young boy with bright red hair. I realize I didn't even ask the man what he thought about the meaning of life. Then again, most of the answers I had gotten were interesting enough, even with their basic notations.

"Is that right? That is very interesting." Almost as if reading his mind, I can tell he is very displeased with this realization. His demeanor has changed from being open to the conversation to closed off and distant. "What makes you so special?" Azazel asks himself; as he looks deep into my eyes, he looks behind him as we both hear footsteps breaking the silence of the sands; the man they call Aerial walks forward into the light of the burning fire.

"He has just told me what he plans to do in the next few days," he says, looking at the ever-turning world. "We tried to make it work," he says quietly. "He just relieved me of my position," he says, sitting across from Azazel. "Now it is time for me to go as well. You're safe for now," he says, pointing at Azazel. "As are you," he says, looking over at me. He exhales a long tired breath. "For a minute there, I thought this would last," he laughs. "But I suppose some part of me knew this would happen at some point," he says as tears fall from his eyes. He holds his hand towards me. I take it in a tight grip and shake the man's hand. It's disheartening to me, as far as I am aware, this man has never made a mistake, and yet he finds himself on the doorsteps of meeting an eternal slumber. "Im Aerial, gatekeeper of The Beyond. I should say I was the gatekeeper," Aerial says, hysterically laughing. "I always thought I would be ready for the day all this would be gone, I gotta tell you. I'm afraid," he says, looking at the both of us. Azazel keeps his cold demeanor by brushing off the statement.

"You shouldn't be," I say softly. "Fear will only make leaving a worse experience for you. Find comfort because you will go home to the stars. Where you will fly higher than the rest of us ever will, as far as I'm concerned, you and Azrael are the only stars up there that will burn brighter." I say, smiling at this man as his body begins to fade away with the wind. He looks at me as if in comfort with his fate.

"I see now why he chose you," Areial says with one last smile as he falls in line with the stars. Azazel gets off the ground and dusts himself off.

"I better be off now," Azazel says, whipping away the snot which hangs under his nose. "I need some time to myself," he says, walking back into the large brush of weeds. My eyes follow him closely as he disappears. After I am sure he is gone, I lie on the soft sand and force myself to sleep. I wake up seeing that the island has become one large dune. The opening to the ridge has become five times larger than it originally was. I quickly get onto my feet, rush to the top of the hill, and look out into The Other, now divided into six different sections. The three in the middle are the smallest. The roads breaking away from one another, twisting and turning to the opening to The Beyond, I see all the islands converging into what I assume to be what historians would call Pangea, the land large in mass. I stumble back down the ridge, run to the ocean, and close my eyes as my feet reach the water. I see a large group of thirty people a few miles away to the right of the opening to the ridge. I rush, pushing against the waves. I reach the shore tripping over myself, causing me to tumble into a rolling fall. I punch the ground before returning to my feet and break into a long-striding run down this eternal beach, hardly leaving any room to breathe the fresh air surrounding this land. Finally, I reach the sizable confused group of people before the sun strikes noon. I wave them down as I bend over and heave out a large pool of vomit. This vomit lies primarily in clear liquid and small chunks of what is left of the squirrel. I look up at the group, who all back up a few feet uncomfortably. I look at the large group feeling small chucks fall into the soft sand from my chin.

"Sorry about that," I heave out, holding my stomach as a burning pain reaches the surface. I take in several sharp breaths and swallow a large pool of that vomit, causing me to quickly bend forward and hold my stomach; as more comes flowing out, I struggle to stand straight as I look at this large group of people. "Ready?" I ask the group, and all nod, agreeing, "Good. Everyone, keep up with me, please." I say, turning around and taking them to The Ridge at a reasonable pace. After they all had gone, I decided to lie down against one of the tallest trees on this land. I lay here, arm over my stomach breathing sharp painful breaths as I plead for my job to be finished for one day.

"Rough day," Azazel says from the weeds. He comes out of the weeds carrying two water bottles. I chuckle and look up at him.

"No fucking shit," I say, taking one of the bottles. "Where did you get these?" I ask, removing the blue lid and drinking the bottle until it is half full.

"You can find just about anything anywhere when you are in this place. Where I come from is full of things left behind from Yesteryear. I ran into a stagecoach just before coming here. There are cities, stores, mountains, and skyscrapers left there in the gray mist of The Other. Yesteryear makes progress. It's left to The Other to take the shambles of a broken world and build itself up from scratch. It's quite nice once you get used to the gunfire and the smell of death hanging in the air," Azazel says, taking a long cool sip from his bottle; he laughs to himself. "It's a bad line of work you've gotten yourself into, mister Dark. Maybe you and I don't get such a nice cookie-cutter ending as they have." He says, taking a longing look up at the blue sky above. "I always wondered what these times would be like," he says with a soft smile. "Honestly, I like knowing how all this will end. It gives me something to look forward to." I take a long breath.

"I had children once. They were both little at the time of my death. Therefore, they didn't understand why their daddy would leave them for a quest leading to nothing. Obviously, they were confused about the whole ordeal. They constantly berated their adoptive parents for not returning me from the psychiatric facility. I made a new friend there who I am uncertain still lives. His name was Michael, the good doctor. They were kids; they didn't understand the primality of death, which, in my case, was not peaceful. I ended so many lives in one month that it's sometimes hard to remember what it was like before I lost my way. I shot a man, crashed a truck belonging to one of my only friends at the time, and killed him too. After my death, I came here but didn't get to watch my children grow up. They will die without me. Move on without me. Such as life goes. I hope my children will grow up to be fine people, and I will be proud of them, even though I already am, because they were strong. My wife, Brittany, will never see them again until it is their time to float on that great ocean. Maybe they already have." I tell myself as tears stream down my cheeks, Azazel watching me intently. "She believed in a permanent marriage though she considered the idea of getting a divorce. Even after death, love is the only thing we will have left of one another, and I like the idea that she still loved me in the end despite all that I had done." I look up at the young man, half asleep from the conversation; I chuckle, wiping away my tears. "What about you? What will you miss about this place?" I ask him.

"The way things used to be. Sure, we were all still young and foolish at the time, but Aerial would come down from that big boy chair he would often put himself into and pay us short visits. We would watch each summer solstice as the northern lights would make stunning movements in the night sky. It was good back then. I miss them, though I guess I have to live with the fact they are both gone now, and there isn't anything you or I could do about that," he says.

"No, I suppose not," I say. I never considered Azazel would be the one to feel nostalgic. Though when the end times are getting closer each day, I suppose it has brought that side out. The side he had hidden from both Azrael and Aerial. I wish they could be here to see this. But, I suppose they are sitting up amongst the bright stars, like the Vincent Van Goh painting from so long ago in Yesteryear.

"Guess we both are still here for something. In the end, that's all that matters anyways." Azazel says coldly. "I better get back to The Other. You have a good night Samuel," he says, clapping my shoulder before retreating into the brush of weeds.

"I suppose we are here for some reason, though only one of us doesn't wish for this place to die," I say as I snuff out the flame and lie down for the night.

CHAPTER SIXTEEN

Brittany, I think to myself, waking up from a restful sleep. Two more days left, I think to myself as I get the ground and dust off my backside. Two more days till all of this is gone. What will become of this place after Azazel, and I take our place amongst the stars? I walk briskly out to the ocean feeling its calm waves splash against the lower part of my legs. I dip my left hand into the water, feeling the tiny fish swim around my fingers.

"It's quite nice out here, isn't it?" says a soft voice coming up from behind me, breaking the silence to which I and the ocean have grown accustomed. "When I first discovered this land, I thought it was merely a peaceful dream in which neither you nor I can escape, and you are fine with this. Why?" he asks curiously. I do not have to open my eyes or turn to recognize the voice of The Beyonder.

"Because I don't want to escape. I don't think I deserve any fate that is any better than the one I received in Yesteryear," I say, remembering how cold that chair felt as I sat down.

"Then why do you not accept what you have done and move forward?" He asks softly.

"Because what I have done shouldn't be accepted. I have no reason to think otherwise, so I hold onto my pain for the remainder of my time in this place. My family is gone now, and I can accept that I may be stuck here for eternity. I may end with the world here. I am fine with that, but I cannot go into The Beyond until I feel as if I am ready to go into that warm comfort, we like to call being at peace if I don't find that. I am fine with being trapped in eternal nothing," I say, finally opening my eyes to turn to this man. "It is my fault that I am here, so it is up to me to decide when I leave. It should be my choice, not yours, or anybody else should make it for me." I say with a cold stare into his light green eyes, which hold a tremendous amount of love and some amount of compassion.

"You say you cannot accept your decisions though you didn't make them consciously," he says questioningly.

"Because you made me like this, you fucking son of a bitch! Why? Why did you do this to me? Why did you make a monster? What was your end goal with me? I deserve an answer!" I scream, staring at this man dead in his green eyes. "I killed my wife!" I say pleadingly.

"Yes, you did. I am sorry, Samuel," he says, taking a few steps back and giving me some breathing room. "I didn't want this for you," he says admittedly. "You seek an answer for why I made you? You do not ask this because you are curious. You ask because you seek someone to blame for what YOU did. Samuel, you seek an answer for why you are the way I wanted you to be, and I am the first to tell you there is no simple answer to anything I do. I know I have led you to believe it, but I have no reasons behind anything I have done, and I apologize for misleading you. Find comfort in that whatever I have done, I did it out of love. Samuel, you did those things initially because you were born to do them. This was your fate from the beginning; this very conversation is fate. It was written in the stars from the beginning. I chose Billy to die because it was his time, as were Nancy and Sandys. They served their purpose. Your wife was also among those who served their purpose to get you here, this moment," he says in a cold fit of anger though I can feel the restraint.

"What now?" I ask scarcely, "What is my place in all this?" The man smiles and turns to the ridge. I ball my fist.

"That I have yet to say. I'm still figuring out how any of us fit into all of this," The Beyonder says, waving his arms wide, suggesting that he is talking about The Sands and the people that reside there. "I will warn you of something, though, do not befriend Azazel, though his temptations seem promising and full of truth. He is a liar and a deceiver who will stop at nothing to get across that ridge," he says, pointing to the top.

"Why tell me this? Why not just let me fall like the others?" I ask hesitantly, loosening my hand, knowing I cannot win in a fight with this man.

"Because, though I am remorseful and forgiving, I cannot forgive him for what he has done to the people of Yesteryear and me. I also quite like you. You are good company when you wish to carry out conversations like this. Sometimes it is good to talk to people." He says with a bright grin.

"Can I ask you something? Why now? Why end things when they are just getting started for them?" I ask.

"Because I love all of my children, and it is time for them to finally come home," he says, staring at the world he had built as if in awe at its beauty. "I will miss moments like these. It reminds me of art in motion. There is nothing like it in the entire universe I have created. This one is so much more special to me than the others, it is my first home, and now I believe it is time for me to say my goodbyes." He says, continuously smiling.

"You love the place, don't you?" I ask.

"Do you not love your creation of Yesteryear? You asked a fascinating question in one of your final written words, *What is value?* Indeed, the answer behind everything that is the universe will never be found without telling a lie or two. However, I would like to think that value is not the purpose of a thing or someone. Value is what Yesteryear was to you. It has many meanings upon many different definitions and cultural beliefs. It depends on the person's perspective, like you. For example, you stated that Yesteryear, or Lucy as you call it, is like a mother that lies. Other people may say something entirely different, and I like that about people. Then again, I enjoy people overall," he says, laughing at his joke. I do not share this same amusement though I find comfort that he is very open. Not many are honest about this sort of thing. Then again, what do I know? I am but a fool. "I believe there are more waiting for you somewhere on the island's South side," he says, pointing in that direction. "I would join you, but unfortunately, I have other pressing matters to attend to," he says slowly, crossing the ocean.

"All right," I silently say to myself as I do the same and walk to the South to collect my quota while being sure to hide my rage; that's all it is at this point, me working a job for a failing business that was a very successful enterprise in its later years. Catching a glimmer of all twenty tall figures took me a few hours. I remember asking one of them how tall they were. This man told me he was precisely six foot ten inches which I found very impressive and quite frightening as I began to realize this tall, hulking figure could have stomped me down to a flat pancake. But, of course, I laughed at this, causing him to become angry. So now I walk back to camp in low spirits and with a bruised jaw which I shouldn't complain about, considering it was my wrongdoing that caused the bruise to appear in such a lively manner.

"Seems you found one of the newest Others for me to collect," Azazel says, coming out of the tall brush of weeds carrying an ice pack. "Figured you would need this. That boy sure has a temperament. I'm going to have fun with him these next two days." He says with a horrifying grin spread across his face. "It's a good time for business," he says as I press the ice harshly against my aching jaw. "We're supposed to have over eight billion people coming over that ridge, and only seventeen million will choose The

Other over salvation; what a bunch of damn fools your people are." He says, chuckling to himself as he looks out past the ocean watching as the sun sets.

"They tried," I say quietly, my voice muffled by the ice pack.

"I'm sorry?" he says questioningly. I remove the ice pack.

"I said they tried. They tried making things work, but then they had to start that mess with another war. I suppose our friend got tired of seeing so many people die for a pointless reason. He got tired of seeing them destroy his perfect gift," I say.

"Perfect," he says smugly. "There is nothing perfect about anything in that place. You are foolish to think that building skyscrapers on top of bodies are perfection," he retorts.

"Never figured you to be the type to care," I say, letting the pain sit momentarily because the ice has grown too cold for my jaw to handle.

"I don't care. Your definition of perfect is somewhat null, don't you agree?" He says, folding his arms over one another and leaning against the tree beside mine.

"Every definition written or told is based on the opinion of who wrote the word or came up with it. It's all about perspective when it comes to that. The world is full of one-sided opinions and cultural beliefs that we never take into account others which is foolish not only for them but for us as well. Sure, it is not a perfect world full of imperfect people, but that is its perfection of it. It is perfect but not perfect in the slightest. If the world was inherently perfect, there wouldn't be any reason behind it." So I say, suddenly realizing that my search for an answer has finally ended. I'm here to forgive myself for my wrongdoings though I cannot.

"Never really thought about it like that," he says admittedly.

"No one ever does," I say coldly. "We humans are so clouded by our earthly desires that we fail to see the bigger picture until it's too late, which we both know is very soon." I hear him grab something from the weeds but ignore it, thinking it is another ice pack.

"Yes," he says, smashing a massive rock against the back of my skull. I scream in pain as I jump from my seating position and fall flat onto the sand.

"Oh, my young friend, you should have seen this coming sooner or later," Azazel says. I hear a hard object fall to the ground and more rustling in the tall weeds. "You killed my friends," he says, coming out of the weeds carrying a long, tall stick. He hurries over as I continuously try to crawl away. Finally, he turns me over onto my back and presses the bar down onto my neck. "I won't let you take me!" I scream for this man to stop this madness, but I am blocked out by the sound of my crushed windpipe, causing me to spit out blood. "What makes you so special, huh? The only thing I see in your pretty little eyes is fear," he says, whispering into my ear. I close my eyes.

THUD, I hear, and I wake up coughing blood. I look over and see Azazel lying on the ground. Then, I look over and visit The Beyonder carrying the same rock Azazel hit me with.

"Is he?" I say, leading into a coughing fit which causes the man to rush to my side, giving me some water that rests at the bottom of a hand-crafted bowl made from rock.

"No, not yet anyway. Don't try to speak. Just drink." The Beyonder says, pouring the water down my throat. "This should heal your lungs. You can talk after you are certain it works." The Beyonder says, lying my head down quickly on the sand. I watch in fear as Azazel gets back onto his knees. "Must I hit you again?" The Beyonder asks, gripping the rock tightly. Azazel looks at us both, the right side of his face drenched in his blood; he smiles and chuckles brokenly.

"No, I think I'm done." He says through laughter. "That was one hell of a hit, old friend," he says admiringly; he looks down at me and closes his smile. "I almost got you," he says, giggling. "I almost did," he says, looking to the stars and back down to The Beyonder, who looks at this man in disappointment and contempt. "You know I don't like it when you look at me like that." He says, looking back up to the stars. "Is it time for me to be with them?" he asks curiously.

"No," The Beyonder says coldly. "You do not deserve that right. You will be erased from this place and be sent somewhere with no stars and no place to run. It will just be you, alone forever," he says coldly. "We do not attack our own, you know this," he says disapprovingly, like a mother would talk if their child broke the window with a baseball.

"The Dark, you're sending me there. I suppose I deserve this fate. But, before you ask Samuel, yes, I am content with my decisions in Yesteryear, and I am very much ready to live with the consequences of my decisions. All that time, all that work for nothing, it doesn't matter; none of this does. I hope I will be better in the next life," he says confidently.

"There will be no next life. Not this time," The Beyonder says. I look at him curiously.

"Oh, I guess I should have seen that coming. Do you know something funny? I actually believed you when you said it would be different this time. Look where your broken promise got us!" He laughs as I look at him questioningly. "It will be different. That was a good one, old friend," he says as he disappears to nothing but the imprint in the sand. The Beyonder watches coldly as the remains of Azazel fade into nothing. The Beyonder faces me.

"Rest; you will be fine by morning, your voice will change, but you should be fine. Do you understand me?" The Beyonder says, looking down at me. I nod, agreeing. "Good man. Now get some rest. We both will be swamped tomorrow," he says, walking away. I ignore this and look up at the stars. Samuel, what have you gotten yourself into? I question myself as my eyes close. Brittany, I'm sorry. I wish you were here to tell you what a fool I was. I want to see our children young again. I want to know how things were before I was this way. Maybe I have always been like this. Things would have been different for all of us if I had seen it sooner. I wish I had been better. I wake up with these thoughts, still swimming and crashing into the side of their separate roads and avenues.

I attempt to scream, but my voice comes out broken and cracked. "Suppose this is how I speak for the time being," I say as I walk up the beach and collect the large group of people. Some come without hesitation, looking forward to meeting their eternal slumber or whatever comes after all this is over. I think of Brittany as we travel through these great planes and the heroine desert where I now reside alone. I find myself thinking of her smile as I lay here catching a raspy breath, and I look out to Yesteryear. I wish I could save it, I wish I could see my children again. Though I am almost sure they have joined their mother in The Beyond. I find comfort in that. Tomorrow is when The Beyonder announces his cataclysm. Tomorrow; what a world shall it be tomorrow, I think, singing to myself in a hardy tune. The song Forever flashes.

"You can break my heart forever if you want to. I'll play the part of the fool" I laugh at my ignorance, the laugh coming out with some trouble as it pains me. "Oh Brittany, what I wouldn't give to see you and our children again," I say, watching as the sun sets on its final days of Yesteryear. I'm glad they never discovered the reason behind my death when they were younger (and full of color). Children take things on and fully bring themselves into the feeling of sadness or regret with thoughts of maybe they should have been a better boy or girl. They take the gravity of the situation and triple it while doing so. I am pleased with the idea that she protects them in The Beyond. "I hate to think they turned out like me in the end," I say, grabbing a small rock from nearby.

I won't bother with making a fire, I think to myself as I throw the rock as hard as possible, only for it to land halfway down the beach.

"Damn," I say, leaning against one of the tallest trees and watching as the stars come and go as darkly silhouetted clouds float under them. "Perfect," I say, smiling at the night sky and the feelings it brings about. Hope, Wonder. With these things in mind, I lay down for a restful sleep, my fingers digging deep into the cold sands. I wake up feeling something kick the bottom of my left heel, and my eyes rise and fall until I decide to sit up. Yawning as I stretch out any tight muscles, I look up and see my newfound friend.

"Is it time?" I ask this man, who watches as the world slowly turns.

"Yes, it is," he says quietly. "It's hard, you know. Seeing something you worked on for so long, something that, for all that you are, disappears into oblivion. I am proud, though. I am rarely a proud man, but this," he points to the world. "But all of it is my justification. The lands, the people, everything about this place represents all the best parts of me. Even though there are troubles and doubts, I have them too. I hope they will know I did it out of love," he says as I stand beside him, watching the sun grow brighter. "You might want to turn around and block your vision," he suggests, turning around himself, facing away, and covering his eyes. I do the same. I jump at the sound of the world imploding in on itself as it touches the sun's atmosphere. For a moment, I almost believe I can hear all their cries for help as they are engulfed in flames. We both turn around simultaneously and look on, seeing that the universe is now gone. "They will be arriving soon," he says as the waves stop as if they two have met their end. I turn to look to the ridge seeing that it is flat ground. The Other, gone like the trees and the bank, the rising dunes are also halted. I squint my eyes and see a large white door at the end of this long road, the door itself a bright color white.

"Is that?" I ask The Beyonder as I turn to face the ocean and watch in awe as bodies surface cold and unscathed; the man turns to me and smiles, holding his hand out to the water, which brings all those billions of people to the surface.

"I'll make your part of the job easy," he says, motioning his hand by a mere inch, and the waves begin to rise and fall once more, bringing all the bodies onto the shore. All lie in the sand, lifeless and untethered to their own consciousness. "Time to wake our new friends," he says with a smile as they all awaken, dazed and confused.

"What is this?" a woman asks a few meters away.

"Where the hell are we?" asks another. The Beyonder walks over, standing in front of a crowd that spans miles.

"I don't know what you plan on doing here," I say questioningly. The Beyonder looks at me, giving me a golden smile that would make anyone believe everything will be alright.

"Hello, friends. As written, you are all welcome home." The Beyonder says, his voice picking up in conflict as if standing inside a deep cavern. "Do not fret, I am but a weary traveler such as yourselves. Nevertheless, you are all finally welcome home. I will show it to you," he says, turning to face what once was the ridge and takes a long stride forward. The large group of people does not move. "Do you not wish to reach salvation?" the man asks the group; a woman steps out of the crowd.

"Where are we going?" She asks, carrying an angry gaze. I back from the group and shove my hands deep into my pockets. This is my last day here; I think to myself worryingly. I will no longer exist. I walk briskly away from the group without any attempts from the others to try and stop me. I go as far as I can before collapsing. I wake up and look at the sky, seeing it has kept its cold dark color.

"I was wondering when you would wake up," The Beyonder says, standing a few feet from me. I sit up to face this man.

"Are you going to send me with them?" I say, pointing to an empty sky.

"Why would I?" he asks curiously, stepping forward and sitting cross-legend.

"Do I not deserve the same fate for what I have done in Yesteryear? Or do I deserve the same fate as Azazel?" I ask, looking at this man's warm face for any sign of anger and finding nothing. Why does he not wish to send me to The Dark or the skies with Ariel and Azrael?

"Are you content with your decisions?" he asks as if he were himself, Azrael.

"I'm not," I retort.

"Would you like to walk with me?" he says as he gets back onto his feet, holding his hand out to me to take.

"I would," I say, taking his hand and getting onto my feet. So we let go and started our walk back to the ridge.

"What is the problem?" he asks.

"There are many things I wish I could have changed," I say. "I wish I was better. Not only as a person but as a husband and a father to my children," I say.

"We all make mistakes, Samuel. If you were made to be a certain way, that would take the fun out of watching you grow into the man you are here. You must learn to deal with what you have done and move forward despite it being unforgiving. You, my boy, are a complex soul. You are so concerned with how I made you. You figured out your reason for being here. Why can't you accept that there is no changing the past? You may think you want to change them, and if I could let you, I would. But, you see the problem now, and making up for that is the grand scheme of the thing. You have taken lives, sure, but you have also led many to a peaceful slumber. Why can't you have that same gift?" He says as the doorway to The Beyond shows. We both fall silent until we reach the straight empty road.

"Because I never asked for this. Any of it! I wanted to die because I thought I deserved to, and what you suggested shouldn't be in the cards for me. What if I'm not ready to leave this place? This place has slowly become my fortitude. The only place left where I can sit and remember all the pain that I brought upon others because I deserve to remember," I ask this man as he takes several steps on the trail.

"Then I will let you make your peace with what you have done, and maybe you will find that you, Samuel James Dark, deserve the right to feel at ease. Then, after you are done, meet me at the door, and I will reveal what you seek." He says, turning back to the trail and strolling to the door as I turn myself and sit cross-legged.

"All this time spent in Yesteryear and now here. Am I ready to forgive myself for all my wrongs and troubles?" I laugh softly. "This is it? Finally, the ending of the story untold. Knowing the inevitable has finally come to pass me by is sad. It's time, Samuel. You can't change what is done. I don't know if I can forgive myself for my actions. But knowing they are all right fills me with joy." As I draw my rendition of what a city is into the sands of land so distant from my own, I see it as my home. "Yet something good came out of all this pain and suffering. The ones I have taken can rest easy, and I hope they will find peace. Hope. I suppose I should thank you for that, Nancy." I say, drawing a swirl around the tallest tower. "Samuel Dark, you have finally managed to do it," I say, smiling and staring at the drawing in the sand, taking in the curvature of the swirls and the imperfect buildings below. An hour flies like a hummingbird rushing home to its family as I contemplate my decisions from Yesteryear. "You have come back to reality," I say as I get onto my feet and walk over to The Beyonder, who looks at me with his brightest grin.

"Are you ready?"

"Yes"

"Good. Have you come to peace with who you are and what you have done? "

"Knowing they are now resting easy, with no pain nor suffering, will help me come to peace."

"Good, go ahead and open that door; they will be waiting for you on the other side," he says, disappearing. I wrap my hand around the doorknob.

"Goodbye, Lucy. May you rest easy knowing you have kept your promise of a better world," I say, opening the door. I smile as I see my family. Then, I close my eyes, feeling like a million pounds have lifted out of my body. I smile, welcoming that extraordinary warmth of being accepted to the Beyond.

I have come back to reality.

December 2022 - January 2023

AUTHOR'S NOTE

I first wrote this novel when it was nothing but a short story from when I had reached a low point in my teenage years. I was very depressed at this time and often went through a phase of self-deprecation. I know this story will not be for everyone, and that is the point. I will leave up the overall meaning of this story for interpretation. Thank you, reader, for deciding to read my tale of Yesteryear, my perfectly twisted poem that I would not change for the world. My Yesteryear – SJ